I0674479

Smig's New Gig

by K. Mizer

Adult Readers Only

SMIG'S NEW GIG

Published by Bewere Books
Flagstaff, Arizona
https://www.bewere.us

ISBN: 978-1-62475-181-3
Printed in the United States, United Kingdom, or Australia
First trade paperback edition: July 2023

Cover art by Tabsley
Edited by Rayah

For my Significant Other.

I'm not sure why you let me write this disaster of a book instead of getting a real job,
but I'm very happy that you did.

Now we can look forward to a lifetime of awkward conversations when people ask what I do for a living.

I think I'll stick with:
"No-good freeloading bum who just sits in the house and plays video games all day."

That sounds respectable.

Chapter 1
The Acquisition

The first inkling that Alexander Smig had that today was going to be somewhat unusual was the sound of someone knocking on his door first thing in the morning. This unexpected occurrence roused him, bleary-eyed and confused. There were not many people who would knock on his door. Alexander had no real family to speak of, his father being deceased and his mother estranged. He had an aunt, but she was something of a black sheep who had moved to Tasmania when he was 14 and hadn't sent so much as a Christmas card ever since. It was highly dubious that the handful of friends he had from the bar would know where he lived, much less show up for a visit unannounced. Besides, living on the second floor of a modest apartment building, someone would have needed to buzz any visitors inside, and all of his neighbors would probably have told them to get lost.

Groaning, he dragged himself from his couch and straightened his shirt as much as he could be bothered to. His brain ran through the most likely offenders on autopilot. Since the building's superintendent avoided being seen by the residents at any and all costs, Alexander's only guess at this point was that one of his neighbors was here to complain about something.

"No, Mrs. Dimpwell," Alexander mumbled. "Just because you let your damn cat out and he doesn't come back in precisely half an hour does not mean that I've kidnapped him for soup."

Staggering half-awake to the entry, he decided he couldn't be bothered to mush his face against the peephole and simply flung the door open.

"Good Afternoon, Sir and/or Madam!" a strange voice greeted him.

Alexander was not especially prepared to meet anyone, but he was *absolutely* unprepared to meet whatever was standing in front of him. It wasn't any of his usual neighbors, the trio of Girl Scouts that somehow managed to keep sneaking in to sell cookies, or even Mrs. Dimpwell's cat. For lack of a better description, it looked like a gigantic lima bean that came up to his waist. It even had that pale green sort of color. Unlike most lima beans, this one was capable of movement, which it demonstrated by shifting itself around, ostensibly for a better view up at Alexander. However, this action was apparently pointless as it clearly lacked anything that could be recognized as a real eyeball. In lieu of this, it sported three large craft googly-eyes just straight up cello-taped onto what could be called its head.

About the only recognizable feature it had was an opening that seemed to be roughly analogous to a mouth. Indeed, that's where the sound had come from when it had addressed Alexander. Yet even this was somewhat off, since its voice seemed to be noticeably out of sync with its vocal movements, like a badly dubbed foreign film. It also had a rather odd triangular hat perched on top of its head and a striped necktie worn backwards around its middle like a cape.

The lima bean spoke again with an enthusiastic and cheery flourish.

"I surmise from various details, such as relative time period, geographic location, cultural norms, physical appearance, and good old-fashioned profiling, that you would be considered a Madam!"

Alexander blinked. He was not, and never would be, awake enough to deal with this situation, and he had a growing suspicion that he wasn't even awake to begin with.

"Um. Well... actually, I think I would be a sir."

"Ah, yes! I'm joking, of course!" The... *individual* before him quipped, giving the unmistakable impression that it hadn't been joking.

"Humor! Yes! Anyhow, allow me to introduce myself. I am a telepholographic projection of Yerligam Snauper of Glunt, acting envoy to Earth. May I bother for you to come in and have a moment of my time?"

It took a long moment for Alexander to try and work out what this little green weirdo was asking. He didn't succeed, but at least he tried.

"For me... to come in?" He asked in confusion.

"Splendid! Many thanks," the envoy replied, apparently pleased with its communication skills.

Without another word, the alien wandered around Alexander and into the apartment. The supposed envoy did not have legs with which to walk but rather perambulated with two long, strange limbs that looked like a coiled spring whose ends were both connected to the rest of its body. The coils rippled in waves, reminiscent of a caterpillar or maybe some kind of sea cucumber. Wandering into the kitchenette, the strange guest assumed a position, possibly what it thought of as 'sitting.'

Alexander stared for a moment at the envoy, then squinted for a brief, dumbfounded minute at the empty hallway. Deciding that he needed to take it a little easier at the tavern from now on, he closed the door and wandered over and sat at the breakfast bar, hoping that this was just some kind of weird dream. The envoy turned to face him, although the googly eyes (one of which had been hastily removed to make a total of two) were pointing everywhere but straight.

There was an awkward silence for a while until Alexander decided to poke the bear.

"Can I get you anything, mister, um... Yearlie-Gam-Snope?"

"Yerligam Snauper of Glunt, but you can call me Ysggun, for short. I don't require anything right now."

"Cool."

"I would suppose you're wondering as to the purpose of my visit!"

"Sure," Alexander said, without meaning it. "That's a thing."

"Well, allow me to congratulate you for being among the latest acquisitions of the Federation of Everything! Earth just capitulated about 0.009 yelaageroos ago."

"Federation of... F-O-E? Foe?"

"We prefer to pronounce the acronym 'phooie.' Yes, and *I* have been commissioned to help incorporate you and your fellow inhabitants into the Federation! I was chosen in no small part for my uncanny resemblance to humans, you know!"

A fly in the apartment buzzed above their heads. The envoy took Alexander's incredulous silence as a sign to continue.

"At this very moment, relative to the rotation of your planet and the customary waking times of your populace, I am being projected before every individual to aid each of you in your transition to placement in the Federal Unified Citizenship Hierarchy. Are you ready to get signed up?"

By this point, Alexander had come to the conclusion that he was either still asleep or had unintentionally consumed something other than alcohol last night. He'd stopped experimenting with drugs a long time ago, but some of the guys he worked with were known to slip things into drinks as a prank. Deciding that food wasn't the worst idea, he slid over a can of nuts and popped open the lid.

"Sure," he said, tossing a handful in his mouth.

"Excellent! Let me begin by saying tha-"

The envoy was interrupted by a blood-curdling shriek from out in the hallway. Nuts shot out across the counter and bounced into every nook and cranny of the kitchen as a very startled Alexander barely managed to stay seated on his stool.

"What the hell was that?" He said reflexively, scrambling for support.

"Ah, you Earth people have interesting ways of greeting envoys. Mister Susan Dimpwell in the nearby apartment is being quite vocal with my telepholographic associate there. Now, as I was starting to say-"

"God, I'm starting to think this isn't a dream," Alexander said, coming to grips with reality and the counter.

"Of course not!" The envoy proclaimed cheerfully. "If I may explain-"

Alexander, momentarily forgetting the giant lima bean in his kitchen, spun around with his remote and turned on the television. A few channel flips brought him to a news anchor, who was trying his best to ignore a perfectly identical Yerligam Snauper of Glunt standing next to him.

"-and reports of this supposed 'envoy' are currently coming in from across the globe."

The perfect replica next to the anchor milled around, evidently trying to get his attention.

"Excuse me!" It peeped, just barely audible on the studio mics.

"Scientists currently appear to be clueless as to how these self-described projections are apparently being broadcast to every single person on the Earth. We go live now to Melissa Macy, who is discussing this perplexing issue with an expert."

The screen now cut to an on-the-scene reporter standing next to another Yerligam Snauper of Glunt. In the background, a flabbergasted man was talking excitedly with yet another Yerligam Snauper of Glunt.

"-ignoring the problem of sending that much energy through the atmosphere, there are so many problems with just timezones alone!" the man in the back exclaimed while pulling out his hair.

"Thank you, Andrew!" Melissa chimed in. "I'm here with Professor Downey of the Extraterrestrial Research Center of Frostbank, Minnesota, who is currently struggling to comprehend this turn of events. Professor? Sir, could I have a word?"

The reporter now tried ineffectively to dig her way into the argument being had over the rotational velocity of the Earth and the inconvenience of night owls. Alexander watched the spectacle unfold as his mind struggled to accept that this was the real, waking world. Suddenly, and without warning, the television screen froze. Alexander, shaken from his trance, looked around. The fly above him hung suspended in mid-air halfway through a flap of its wings. Everything had been frozen still except for himself and the envoy.

"Please forgive the temporary stasis," the envoy piped up. "The F.U.C.H.-ing process is very important, and I think there's a few too many distractions around. If you have no objections, I think we should begin."

Alexander looked at the big lima bean a bit nervously now. The envoy's tone and demeanor were just as cheerful as they had been, but the fact that it could apparently freeze time and space itself on a whim made everything about the lima bean seem more intimidating.

"Okay..." Alexander said. "So, what happens now?"

"First of all, I am happy to inform you that all Earthlings have been designated E-class citizens!"

"Is that good?"

"Only if I don't tell you about the nicer class designations," the envoy gladly proclaimed. "But I won't do that. Yes, E-class citizens are eligible for a selection of rights and freedoms that are quite similar to those that Earthlings are already accustomed to. We're particularly proud of our 'Breathable Air' program. I can provide you with a full list of entitlements if you want."

"Maybe later. Does this mean that you're taking over and changing everything?"

"Oh, we're not implementing any major changes as of yet. The Federation generally prefers a light-handed approach to planetary management. There will be a few small tweaks, such as replacing your vast plethora of government systems with a single automated one, but I'm sure this will have a minimal impact on your day-to-day life. We do realize, however, that even minuscule changes can create potential instabilities. So, we offer an extensive support program for citizens, including our interfederal employment program. I can give you information on that if you'd like to look into opportunities beyond your planet!"

"I see. Well, uh. I've already got a job that I'm pretty happy wi-"

He was interrupted by the jingle of his cell phone going off. Alexander pulled it out and saw that his boss was calling him. The envoy had turned slightly purple, which maybe meant that he was perplexed, but Smig wasn't quite sure.

"Um, you mind if I take this?" Alexander asked.

"That shouldn't be possible," the envoy replied, definitely confused. Alexander went ahead and answered anyway. There was a bit of robotic buzz, but his boss came on almost immediately.

"Alex! Are you there?"

"Yeah, Jerry. I'm here."

"You have the alien guy at your place?"

"Yeah. What the hell is going on?"

"I have no clue, but the higher-ups at corporate freaked out and just dissolved the company. We're all out of a job."

"... *Shit*," Alexander said with disbelief.

"Exactly! And the bums only offered me severance if I called and fired everyone before they have to divvy out the retirement fund."

"Fucking vultures."

"That's what I said. God, I've been wanting to rip Tim Coleman a new one for a long time, and I finally did. That was worth way more than what they were offering."

"Damn straight, wish I could have been there to hear that. What are you going to do now?"

"Well, uh, the truth is, my wife Ellie's been kind of obsessed looking for an opportunity to go full end-of-days, zombie-apocalypse survivor on everyone. She thinks this is it, and I've been trying to talk her out of hiking up into the Alaskan interior. Beyond that, I have no clue what's next. What are you thinking?"

"I have no idea, Jerry. God damn it, I only just woke up less than five minutes ago. I *guess* the alien guy wants to talk to me about some kind of employment program."

"Might not be a bad idea to hear him out, Alex. Seems like everyone on Earth is panicking and sending everything to hell."

"Well, thanks for the heads up."

"No problem, Alex. Hey, listen, I gotta go. I just saw Ellie coming up the driveway with a train of pack mules."

"Alright. Take care, Jerry."

"Yeah, you too."

Alexander hung up and put the phone down. The envoy had pulled out some kind of gadget and was presumably trying to figure out how the call had made it through the 'freeze ray' effect.

"Okay, so it looks like I don't have a job after all," Alexander said, taking a deep breath and rubbing his eyes. "I guess it can't hurt to hear you out on this employment thing."

"Splendid!" the envoy proclaimed, returning to his previous shade of green. "Allow me to bring up the application forms!"

"Oh God," Smig buried his face in his hands and ran them over his head. "Is there a lot of paperwork involved?"

"My good sir, it's the Federation of Everything!" the envoy proclaimed. "Paperwork is our pride!"

Alexander sighed as a newly conjured telepholographic printer was somehow spitting physical sheets out onto the kitchen floor. This was going to be a long day.

Chapter 2
The Paperwork

Several days after the envoy's visit, Alexander had reflected and regretted the decisions leading up to this point many times over. Given the unprecedented upheaval that humanity was undergoing, he was not left with many desirable options. Still, if he had known he'd have to wait for ludicrously long periods of time in waiting areas and fill out whole reams of paperwork (both things he absolutely hated doing), then he may well have decided to find some mules and follow Jerry and Ellie up into Alaska.

As it was, he was sitting in another waiting room. This one was in a building that had been hastily constructed by the Federation and made to look authentically 'Earth-like.' On the surface, it did give the passing impression of the sort of waiting room you might get from a hospital drama, but if you got too close, the flaws started to peel off of the ceiling and land on your face. The magazines were a jumble of random pictures and words, the water cooler was a single solid piece (including the 'water' inside), but perhaps the strangest of all was that the fake plants were *indeed* fake, but all of them emitted a low, menacing humming noise that never seemed to stop. In particular, one ██████████ *{WOODY EVERGREEN}* in the corner seemed to increase the intensity of its hum if you got too close to it.

An alien secretary sat behind the counter at the far end of the room, staring at a computer screen. Despite Yerligam Snauper of Glunt's insistence on having a close physical resemblance to humans, pretty much every other alien Alexander had seen or encountered in the past few days had been significantly more humanoid. The secretary here even had two arms and two legs, albeit they were arranged front and back rather than left and right.

Alexander had been waiting in line for about half an hour now, and as far as he could tell, the secretary at the front desk didn't seem to be doing anything important. He hadn't always been sure that Earthling secretaries did much either, but at least they made an effort to blink every once in a while. He glanced down at the little piece of paper with his number that was slowly dissolving in his hand, then went back to staring at the customer counter. It had taken him a little while to realize that whoever was in charge of the fixtures had installed the number display upside down.

"At least they got the bathrooms *mostly* right in this one," Alexander thought to himself.

They definitely had not gotten it right in the last Federation building he had waited in. He was doing his best to block that memory when the intercom crackled on.

"Beeeeep," the secretary called out, imitating an electronic chime. "Number 1139. 1139, please come to the counter."

"Finally," he whispered.

Alexander got up and tried to loosen up his stiff joints a bit as he made his way over.

"Hello, number 1139!" the secretary greeted him cheerfully. "I have just a few brief questions while the number ahead of you wraps up."

Alexander gave a weak smile and kept the groaning in his head. He'd learned very quickly that '*a few brief questions*' was, apparently, someone's idea of a joke when you dealt with the Federation. The secretary began to read off of her screen.

"First of all, I see that you made a request to truncate your employment admissions process. Quoted here as: "*What do you mean there's more paperwork? For the love of all that is holy, how much more can*

*there be? I'm sick of it! I swear if you give me another six-inch stack of forms
to fill out, I'm going to take that pile and shove it right up yo-*"

"A-ah, yeah!" Alexander interrupted. "Oh jeez, I'm sorry. I, uh...
lost my temper a little bit at the last office there."

"Not a problem! Are you still seeking to shorten the admissions
process at this time?"

"Yes, if that's possible."

"In that case, I am happy to say that you have been selected
as eligible to participate in our experimental *Fast-Trak-Job-Attak*™
sub-program. This waives any and all nonessential requirements
such as:

*career counseling, negotiation of terms, wage-bidding, qualification exams,
job training, description of duties, declaration of liabilities, application for Union
representation, work-related safety orientation, choice of heart and mind insurance,
eligibility for worker's compensation, initial setup for processing Federal income tax,
and other extraneous aspects of employment processes and procedure.*

However, some career positions are excluded from the sub-program, dropping the total number of qualifying, available openings
from 58,488,322,812 to only 57,836,109,843. Would you still be interested in signing up for the sub-program?"

"If it lets me skip ahead, I'm a-okay with that. Sign me up."

"Wonderful! Let me send off your application."

The secretary paused for only a brief second, staring motionless
at her screen, before turning back to him in one fluid motion.

"Congratulations! I've run your information, and you have been
accepted into the *Fast-Trak-Job-Attak*™ sub-program!"

"Great!" Alexander said, unsure if he was surprised by the speed
or startled by the apparent lack of input on the secretary's part.
"What do I do now?"

"I've gone ahead and canceled any scheduled appointments that
are no longer necessary. I'm going to give you the new, simplified,
and condensed employment application packet. Your task right now
is to read it thoroughly, choose the occupation you wish to apply
for, and return the forms either to this office or fax it to the district
office address on the back."

The secretary pulled out an eight-inch thick envelope and thumped it on the counter. Smig reluctantly hefted it up into his arms. He had enough experience hauling bags of concrete that he figured it had to be at least fifteen to twenty pounds. It wasn't the biggest stack of papers he'd been handed in the last few days, but Alexander still felt a bit of cold sweat coming on.

"Ah, are there, um, a lot of forms to fill out in here?"

"Only a handful! The bulk of this packet is the catalog of available job types, organized alphabetically."

Alexander flipped the flap on the severely overextended manila envelope and peeked inside. Sure enough, a thick paper catalog took up most of the space.

"Cool. So, I already know what kind of job I want to apply for. Can I fill this out here and just hand it back in today?"

"My, aren't you an eager weasel!" The secretary quipped. "Absolutely!"

"Will I need to take another number to hand it in?"

"Nope, just bring it up to the counter when you're done."

"Wonderful! Thank you."

"Thank you, number 1139!" she merrily proclaimed before swiveling back to stare motionless at her screen again.

Alexander returned to a chair and pulled out the catalog. He'd done a few odd jobs here and there, just like anybody else, but construction jobs were as close as he'd ever come to a genuine career. In particular, he liked the low-to-mid range positions that could avoid having to fill out too many forms or answer too many complicated questions. You wound up answering an ungainly amount of dumb ones, but he'd take that over accounting any day. Maybe they didn't pay very well, but there wasn't a job in the world, hell, even the galaxy that could've paid him enough to deal with anything more complicated than a time card.

Flipping through the massive book, he ran his finger down a few pages. There were far more jobs beginning in 'con-' than he could ever have imagined, and they were all printed so small as to be barely legible. Alexander wasn't entirely sure if the Federation had included some of the more outlandish entries because they were unfamiliar with Earthly occupations or if they seriously considered 'Conversationalist', 'Convict', and more worryingly 'Condiment' as legitimate jobs.

Eventually, though, he found the listing for 'Construction Worker – General.' Squinting hard, he copied the ID number for the position onto the proper form. From there, things were fairly straightforward. He listed his old supervisor Jerry as a reference, hoping that he wasn't already Yukon ho, and filled out all the little details he'd done probably a hundred times already.

In a few minutes, he was finished. Smig got up and returned to the counter, triumphantly handing the encyclopedic ream of paper to the secretary.

"Wonderful!" she exclaimed. "I'll have this sent in right away. It may take some time to process, but you should expect a call within 2 weeks. If you haven't heard anything after that or need any other assistance in the meantime, you can get in touch with this office."

Alexander gave a sigh of profound relief and thanked the secretary. He left satisfied that he could relax for a while now that the paperwork nightmare was finally over, at least temporarily. The secretary pulled Smig's paperwork out of the envelope and entered it into the computer, holding each page in front of the screen and making a soft *boop* noise with her mouth. Information was instantly transmitted into databases billions upon billions of light-yelaageroos away through technology and mechanisms far too boring to bother explaining.

There was, however, a problem. Not with the equipment, since that had numerous redundancies and fail-safes to avoid problems, but with the information itself. Whether it was the small print of the catalog, the haste with which Alexander had copied the ID code, the feisty hand of Fate herself looking for stimulation on a dull Wednesday afternoon, or some combination of the three, the wrong code had been registered.

Even worse, the code was a valid one. A valid code for a valid job with valid tax status and free parking at select parkades throughout the known multiverse. So Alexander's application passed through the Federal Unified Central Knowledge Electronic Database, unchallenged by the Nearly Error-less Registry Director. From there, it was stamped, counter-stamped, ratified, leaked in its entirety onto the internet, un-ratified by accident, re-ratified, passed around several board meetings for laughs, misplaced, downloaded from the internet, and finally submitted to the data banks of the Department of Information Collection and Knowledge Hoarding's Executive Administrative Depository of Stuff.

Alexander walked on, blissfully unaware that the job title now being memorized by the Federation's data banks and beta tanks, next to his name and new federal security limerick, was definitely not 'Construction Worker – General.'

Only two days after handing in the paperwork, Alexander received a phone call.

"Alexander Smig?" asked a somewhat gravelly voice.

"Yeah, that's me."

"I'm Grand Master Whoople of the Federal Union of Commissions and Key Employment Resource Supervision. Your job application's been processed, and I'm happy to say that we're ready to take you onto the next step and get you hired."

"Hey, fantastic! What happens now?"

"Well, I see you're on the *Fast-Trak-Job-Attak™* sub-program, so I'll try to keep things as brief as I can, but I have to say that you're applying for a pretty broad field. If it's alright with you, I'd like to ask a few quick questions to help narrow a few things down before we get to a full placement interview."

"Sure thing."

Smig hoped that 'a few quick questions' meant the same thing to this Grand Master Whoople that it meant to him.

"Great! Let me look through my list here. Uh, the big one is to get some idea of your basic physical attributes, so you don't end up being mismatched with anything that's too big, too heavy, or requires the use of more limbs than you actually have. Sound alright?"

"Yeah, that makes sense."

"Okay. And I do want to mention that I'm not quite familiar with Earthlings at the moment, so apologies in advance if I stumble into some unintentionally awkward questions."

"No problem."

"Let's see. According to my notes, most Earthlings conform to a pattern A10-BcQ anthropoid configuration. Is this true for you?"

"Uh, I'm not sure? I mean, I'm not massively different than most people."

"Single torso with 2 arms, 2 legs, and 1 head?"

"Yeah."

"Alright. Could I have your age, height, and weight?"

"31 years old. Six feet, two inches tall. About 180 pounds, give or take."

"Gonna be fun trying to figure out how to convert all of that," Whoople mumbled absent-mindedly. "How about fitness? Could you give me an idea of how strong you are?"

"Well, I did manage to bench press almost 200 pounds the last time I went to a gym, though that was a while ago."

"Any recent injuries?"

"Um, well, I tore a ligament in my leg about a year ago, but that's been healed up for a couple months now."

"Body hair?"

"What?"

"Sorry, do you have any hair?"

"Oh. Uh, yeah. I guess I've got kinda light brown hair. I usually keep it trimmed short. Pretty good at remembering to shave when I need to."

"How many nipples do you have?"

There was a bit of a pause.

"Two?" Alexander answered hesitantly.

"Is that something that can change on Earthlings?" the Grand Master asked in a concerned tone.

"Uh, no. Not unless you lose one in an accident or something, I guess."

"Is that more or less true for most of your physical components? I'm cross-referencing some Earthling samples, and they seem to be pretty consistent."

"Yeah, I should have everything you'd expect in terms of... body parts."

"Okay. No major accidents, alterations, or body modifications?"

"Uh, just a small tattoo on my left kneecap. I, uh, lost a bet in college and haven't managed to do anything about it yet."

"I see. Well, that takes care of a lot of the basics. Just out of curiosity, would you be open to the possibility of certain modifications?"

"Uh... Well, maybe? I don't know."

"Don't worry about it. Running mods can open up all kinds of options, but that's something we can discuss later. Moving on, would you be willing to travel and be absent for extended periods of time for work?"

"Sure."

"Would you be willing to consider moving *permanently* for work, including potentially off-planet?"

Alexander briefly thought that one over. He didn't have much in the way of possessions and even less in terms of relationships tying him down. There were a few friends down at the bar and some construction pals who'd miss him, but none of them were exactly blood relations.

"It's been a while since I've moved around, but yeah. I guess I'm in a good position if there are benefits for relocating."

The Grand Master went through a plethora of similar questions about his willingness to work in hazardous conditions, keep his mouth shut about confidential information, and if he'd compromise any other little particulars. To Alexander, it all seemed pretty standard stuff from human resource departments worried about their workers compromising the company's little particulars. A few were genuinely confusing but not quite on the same level as the nipples, so Alexander more or less shrugged them off.

"Well, Mr. Smig," Whoople concluded. "I think I have everything I need, and I see a potential opportunity to get into a very highly-valued category of work if you're interested. There are a bunch of high-profile clients who spend pretty much all their time traveling from one side of the universe to the other and like to take their own dedicated personnel along with them. They can be a demanding bunch, but they offer some of the best benefits and highest pay across the whole spectrum. Does that sound like something you might be interested in?"

"Maybe. Would that mean I'd be living on some kind of spaceship?"

"More or less, though with the kind of people I'm talking about, it wouldn't just be any run-of-the-mill spaceship. You'd be on board a Federal Cruiser. Practically a small city capable of traveling at speeds incomprehensible to any physicist. Depending on what sort of contract you land, you could end up on something like a Shmrueger Brothers' luxury casino yacht. Let me tell you, that's usually a tough position to get into, but being from an exotic new planet is very attractive to these kinds of employers."

"Well, sounds like it'd almost be foolish to turn down an opportunity like that. What the heck, let's go for that."

"Excellent! Now, I know I sprung the idea on you all of a sudden, but can you estimate roughly how soon you might be able to pack up and be ready to move if you get hired?"

"Uh..."

Alexander did a quick mental count of the things he owned and wasn't leasing in some way. If he hadn't been holding the phone, he'd have some fingers left over.

"Not long," he replied. "I'll need a few days to sort out my stuff at the apartment, but that should be about it."

"That's great! So this is how things are going to work: I've got an early-bird pool of clients getting ready to send representatives to a collective interview. We do that to save having to schedule ten or twenty individual interviews for every candidate, which would get pretty tiring for everyone, as I'm sure you can imagine. You'll need to show up to physically demonstrate your work ability and answer any questions they might have in the moment. After that, there's some haggling behind the scenes, but if anyone's interested, you'll get a handful of contract offers, and you can take your pick. If you can be ready to go in about, uh... where's the conversion rate for Earth time..? Ah! About 1.5 weeks, I can get you into this first round, and I think you've got a good chance of being hired same-day."

"Wow, really?"

"It's a healthy hiring market, and like I said, everyone always wants to snap up a few people from the latest Federal acquisition for novelty's sake."

Alexander couldn't imagine why anybody would hire a construction worker for the sake of novelty, but then again, he'd heard of things like foreign companies hiring Americans just to attend board meetings and look like they've got some sway on the world stage.

"Sounds great!" he said. "I should be ready to go by then."

"Wonderful! From this point going forward, I'm your agent. So, if you have any questions or need to reschedule or something, get in touch with me."

"Sounds good!"

Alexander hung up the phone and started sorting through his stuff.

"Why the hell did they need to know about my nipples?" he thought absent-mindedly.

Chapter 3
The Preparations

Today was the big day. Alexander had managed to divest himself of everything but a single, overstuffed bag of essentials and a small potted Christmas Cactus he hated to get rid of despite the awkwardness of having to hold it now. After a gaggle of phone conversations with Whoople and a few administrative assistants, he had even taken on faith the Federation's promise to put him up somewhere for free during the hiring process and divested the lease on his apartment. Now he found himself waiting in another Federation structure, though things were a little different this time.

The aliens had landed cruisers on Earth in strategic locations on the outskirts of numerous centers of civilization. In the span of a single night, they had plonked down and set up connections to any transportation networks that happened to be nearby. However, the remarkable speed of this logistical construction did not seem to be matched by any ounce of efficiency. News helicopters broadcasted sweeping views of tangled bus lanes and maglev tracks that looked like massive webs designed by the spiders from NASA's psychoactive drug tests crisscrossing hither and yon.

Alexander thanked his lucky stars that the ship he was summoned to had established itself within reasonable walking distance from an existing bus line. There were a few hairy crossings over alien road surfaces that seemed like they were made of some kind of vegetable material, like super-dense broccoli heads, but he managed to navigate to the entrance without getting into an accident or needing to decipher the cryptic transit schedule maps posted at the Federal junctions.

The waiting room Alexander now sat in was still designed with humans in mind, but it had dropped any pretense of looking like something that had come from Earth. In some ways, this was an improvement since it removed the ominously humming plants, but it also felt as if the other waiting room where he had handed in his initial application had simply been renovated. The layout and dimensions were almost identical, the air had that same strange, metallic thinness to it, and Alexander swore that the secretary at the counter was an almost perfect copy of the one he'd handed the packet to, aside from the extra arm of course. He had to keep reminding himself that this wasn't even the same building and was, in fact, a section of a gargantuan Federal space cruiser located miles away.

Alexander had only seen a handful of alien spaceships on the news, and most of them looked like the manufacturer's design departments were all run by very large committees who were well practiced in the art of coming up with compromised solutions to aesthetic challenges. In that regard, this one was no different, but it certainly was vast. It undoubtedly outclassed any vehicle on Earth in terms of size and complexity. Alexander had been lucky to find the right waiting room almost immediately. There were at least twenty open entrances on this side of the ship alone.

"Beeeeep," the secretary called out on the intercom. "Number 1137. 1137, please come to the counter."

It took a second of staring at his ticket for Alexander to realize that this was him. He rushed up to the desk with his bag and cactus in hand.

"Hello, number 1137!" the secretary greeted him cheerfully. "Grand Master Whoople is ready to prepare you for your interview in room DY-101. Here's a map."

She handed him a stylized map printed on a sheet of laminated paper, something like what you'd get for a shopping mall or convention center. Alexander jumped a little when the image shifted on the paper and refocused to draw a line from the reception desk to room DY-101. Part of him was impressed by the technology, but mostly he was intimidated by the sheer number of rooms and hallways on the ship.

"Thanks," he said, still staring at the map.

"Thank you, number 1137!" the secretary said.

Given the magnitude of the massive internal structure, it took Alexander a while to navigate his way around the ship. Not only did the lengthy hallways compare to the road network of a small city, but the onboard gravity system was designed to take advantage of the ceiling and walls as additional floor space. This was undoubtedly a handy feature, but it startled him the first time a group of aliens meandered by only a few inches above his head. At some point during his wandering back and forth through various corridors, the map seemed to take pity on him and gradually dumbed down the directions until he started making consistent progress.

Eventually, he found room DY-101, though whether or not he was still technically on the floor or the ceiling was a bit up in the air. The door slid open to reveal a small space that reminded Alexander of a theater dressing room. A tall, slim alien with dark, purplish blue-grey skin was seated in the corner, mumbling to himself. Alexander's attention was immediately drawn to his big, triangular ears and the subtle series of wavy ridges along his top lip, which made it look like he had a 'Tom Selleck'-esque mustache.

"Alexander Smig?" the alien asked, peering around the bundle of papers stacked on his clipboard.

"That's me."

"Good to finally meet you, Alexander. I'm Grand Master Whoople."

Flashing a somewhat startling smile of sharp-looking teeth, the Grand Master rose and took a mere two steps to meet Alexander at the door, his long, whip-like tail swishing behind him. Whoople couldn't have been much more than a foot taller than him, but it wasn't very often that Alexander had to crane his neck up to look someone in the eye.

"Come on in, Mr. Smig," Whoople said, shaking Alexander's hand firmly as he led him inside. "You can leave your bag in the rhombohedron over there. Have you used one of these before?"

Alexander followed Whoople's gesture to stare at an oddly-shaped cubby set into the wall. You never could tell with the Federation if it was some kind of highly advanced technology or just a plain hole in the wall. Either way, the aliens around him usually seemed quite happy to give him a lengthy, drawn-out explanation, even if it was just a hook to hang his coat on.

"I'm not entirely sure," he answered.

"It's quite simple, actually. Just stick your bag in that oddly-shaped hole in the wall."

"Ah."

Feeling only a little silly, Alexander plopped his bag into the cubby and gingerly set his Christmas cactus next to it. Immediately they disappeared with an audible 'ZWOOP.' He froze, staring at the empty hole that had briefly contained the last of his earthly possessions.

"From there-" the Grand Master continued. "-it's transmitted to one of our super-dense, data compression spheres. I think you call them black holes."

"It just shot my stuff into a black hole?" Alexander asked, now more concerned with the fact that the cubby was big enough for him to fall into.

"Yep. Whenever you'd like it back, you can go up to any Federation storage rhombohedron and ask for it. Should pop right out. Now, we don't have much time before the interview starts, so if there's anything you need, tell me now."

"I, uh... Does this thing have any kind of safety mechanisms?"

"The rhombohedron? I guess it does," the Grand Master answered as if he'd never given it much consideration before. "I've never heard of anyone's stuff getting mangled in transit or anything."

"I kinda meant if there's anything to keep it from sucking me in."

"Oh! Well, I wouldn't go climbing into one, of course, but it's pretty rare for it to get people and possessions confused. I hear they're pretty quick with retrievals if it does happen, though, so don't worry too much about it."

"Okay," Smig said without much relief. "Is my cactus going to be okay?"

"Oh, that'll be fine! Basically puts it in stasis, so you'd have to leave it in there for thousands of yelaageroos, or Earth years even, before it ages to the point where it needs attention. Anyways, we should get this show going. A few of the clients that are here today can be awfully picky about punctuality."

Alexander was only too glad for the Grand Master to lead him away from the rhombohedron and down a long hallway.

"I take it you've never done a Federation-style collective interview like this before."

"No, I haven't."

"It's perfectly natural to be nervous, of course, but it's set up to be as unobtrusive as possible. The clients can see us through the walls, and I've got a mic in my ear to take questions, but you won't see or hear anything from them directly. I'm the only one you're interacting with, and my main job is to make sure you look good in their eyes. This is something I've done a thousand times, Mr. Smig, and I'm on your side. How's your stamina?"

"Um, it's all right," Alexander replied, not entirely sure what he meant.

"Good deal. You don't have to be modest, Mr. Smig. It *is* an interview, after all, but don't worry if you start to flag. Getting a sense of your boundaries is all part of the process; how long you last, your recovery period, that sort of thing. Just relax and take things as they come."

Alexander didn't have much time to mull this over, as they now stopped in front of another door. The Grand Master glanced over his clipboard once more and stared at a panel on the wall with strange symbols that Alexander took to be some kind of alien language.

"Hmm, full crowd already," the Grand Master mused, glancing over to Smig one last time. "You ready for this?"

Alexander took a deep breath.

"As ready as I'm going to be."

"All right, it's show time."

Whoople shoved his clipboard into a smaller rhombohedron in the opposite wall and straightened his clothing before sliding open the door. With the rapid buildup of anxiety, Alexander was almost expecting some kind of auditorium stage with glaring lights. Thankfully, the room was far smaller and more comfortable looking than he had expected. While it may have felt crowded with a few more people, it was perfectly spacious enough for two. It was roughly circular in shape, and the transition from the walls to the floor was obscured by a very low couch custom built to stretch around the entire room. The ambient lighting seemed to come up from behind the top line of the couch, bright enough to be clear but not so intense as to be uncomfortable.

Alexander noted the apparent lack of any obvious cameras, windows, or even interrogation-style one-way mirrors. The knowledge that some unknown number of aliens were watching kept him a little on edge, but the overall atmosphere was strangely more casual than he expected.

The Grand Master strode into the center of the room and briefly addressed the walls.

"Ladies, Gentlemen, and otherwise, welcome! I am Grand Master Whoople, and this is Mister Alexander Smig. With our thanks for your kind patience, we are ready to commence the interview."

The room remained empty and silent, but it was hard to dispel the idea of many hidden eyes now staring intently at them. The Grand Master turned and addressed Alexander directly now.

"Please have a seat, Mr. Smig."

They sat down opposite each other. Given how low the cushions were, Alexander found himself mimicking the Grand Master's relaxed, half-sitting, half-laying position. Whoople rested his hands together on one knee as he began.

"Now, just to start things off, do you prefer being referred to as Mr. Smig? Or would you be more comfortable with some kind of nickname or nom de plume?"

"Oh, um, just Alexander is fine with me."

"Perfect! Now, Alexander, I understand you have a few ye-laageroos in the field, but would you care to elaborate a little on your career as a concubine?"

"Well, i- uh, as a what?"

"Concubine," the Grand Master enunciated. "Or is there another term you're more used to?"

Here he stole a glance at some alien characters that had popped up on the wall next to him.

"Let's see, there's courtesan, partner, 'mister-ess,' escort, paramour, kept man, third wheel, boy-toy, or anything you'd prefer."

Alexander gave Whoople a long blank stare as the gears started grinding in his head. Groaning internally, he bent forward to whisper behind one hand to the Grand Master.

"I, uh... I'm sorry. Can I have a quick word with you? I think there's been some kind of mistake."

"Certainly." The Grand Master whispered back, looking concerned.

"Pardon us for a moment," he said, addressing the walls again. "We won't take long."

Grand Master Whoople led Alexander back through the door to the hallway.

"What's the problem?" the alien asked with concern.

"Let's start with the fact that I *thought* I was applying for a job as a *construction worker.*"

"Ah," Whoople remarked with a dawning expression on his face. "Well, this is *definitely* not the right interview if that's what you're after."

"No kidding. Please, for the love of God, don't tell me that I filled in the wrong ID number and put down concubine instead of construction worker."

"Hang on a second, Alexander, let's have a quick look at the forms you filled out."

The Grand Master tapped a rapid series of finger strokes on the wall screen. Promptly it displayed a copy of Alexander's application paper. Both of them squinted at the job ID number.

"Well, the registry forms definitely have it put down as ıILliı[ılIl} I," he mused. "Though looking at the scan of your physical copy, that closed curly bracket does look more like the number three."

"Yes! Okay, that *was* supposed to be a three," Alexander sighed. "Is that the problem?"

"Well, it certainly appears to be the reason you got mixed around," the Grand Master said thoughtfully. "And it goes a long way to explain the *interesting* conversation I had with the fellow you listed as a reference, but that's not your only problem."

"What do you mean? Is there something dumb, like a contractual obligation to complete the interview or something?"

"Oh, no! Of course not. There's no point if you don't want the job."

"Are your clients going to be angry?"

"Nah, they're mostly politicians and business people. Honestly, they're happy to do just about anything to get away from their constituents and board members for a while."

"So, what's the problem?"

"Well, it was announced yesterday that all construction jobs in the Federation are officially being outsourced to the Bodgers of Rhygon 2. I always figured it'd be another couple billion yelaageroos before they cleared that one, but it sounds like they just discovered that a previous parliament had, in fact, passed the order and didn't bother to tell anybody. Unfortunately, that pretty much means no more construction jobs are going to be available for the foreseeable future unless you happen to be a Bodger, which you aren't."

Alexander considered this a moment.

"Well, that sucks, but maybe I can shop around and try my hand at something else. If I make sure to write clearly, that fast track deal does seem to make things pretty easy."

"The *Fast-Trak-Job-Attak™* sub-program?" Whoople asked.

"Yeah, that one."

The Grand Master tapped the screen again. A dizzying array of alien characters and symbols ran past in a blur. Whoople frowned and sucked air between his teeth.

"They canceled it. As it turns out, throwing under-informed applicants out into an unfamiliar universe with next to no counseling or training was having *'mixed results.'* If you want to apply for a different position, you'll have to go through the regular process again, and *that* looks like it's being flooded with an increasing spike of applicants from your home planet. About 3 billion and counting according to this."

"Judas Priest. That means a hell of a lot more waiting and God knows how much more paperwork, doesn't it?"

"Possibly even more than when you started. They've been frantically subdividing the various agencies involved to accommodate the increasing demand. Doesn't exactly make things go any faster, but it does give you a wider option of waiting rooms you can sit in."

Alexander felt the cold sweat coming back with a vengeance. Something started ringing in the back of his head. For a moment, he felt like one of those war veterans from the movies stuck in a flashback, staring at scores of helicopters flying over 'nam while people screamed off in the background.

"Hey, uh... Crazy idea. Can I keep going?"

"What?"

"Could I keep going with *this* interview?"

"Really?" the Grand Master asked, genuinely surprised. "Are you sure?"

"I mean, if I don't have to go through any more paperwork, I could give concubine-ing? Concubinage?... Being a concubine, a shot. Worst case scenario, nobody hires me, and I have to go straight back to square one anyway. Can I still try out for it?"

Grand Master Whoople studied him seriously for a minute.

"Listen, Alexander, you're darn lucky that the *Fast-Trak-Job-At-tak™* sub-program waives almost all of your requirements. We can still do the interview and try to get you hired, but I wasn't expecting I'd have to work with a complete novice when I got the clients set up. Do you have any idea what being a concubine involves?"

"Not entirely," Alexander admitted. "Aren't they basically like an extra spouse with lower social status?"

"More or less. As a career, the job is to develop a relationship, potentially dealing with a vast range of highly nuanced interpersonal aspects that require all kinds of psychological and emotional training to navigate effectively, but most importantly, it relies on a lot of sex. All intercourse is legally required to be consensual among all parties, of course, but the biggest expectation is that some kind of fooling around will take place at some point. That's exactly why the fast track sub-program skipped all of the boring things like psycho-emotional evaluation, counseling in intergalactic social norms, relationship management training, and those awkward 'get-to-know-you' dinner dates. The main purpose of this interview is to get down to bare bones and see how you do the four-legged foxtrot. They're trying to get an idea of what you're like physically. Do you get what I'm saying?"

"Yes," Alexander replied.

"Are you sure that this is absolutely what you want to get yourself into?"

Alexander took in a deep breath and thought it over.

"What exactly is the expectation here? Like, specifically for the interview."

"They'll want a good look at you without any clothes or non-permanent accessories, and they will expect some kind of sexual activity to be displayed. Depending on what you're comfortable with, there are some bare minimums we could get away with, but if you very much want to take this opportunity seriously, then I would stress the importance of trying to show off as much as possible and hopefully giving them something that will stand out."

"And this sexual activity is going to be demonstrated with you?"

"Yep. That's what Grand Masters do."

"I had absolutely no idea," Alexander said. "Would I, uh... be giving or receiving?"

"If you're willing to do both, that broadens the field of potential takers, but it's entirely down to your comfort zone."

Whoople glanced at the display on the wall.

"I want you to make an informed decision, Alexander, but bear in mind we're keeping some ludicrously powerful and important people waiting on us."

"You're right. Listen, part of me is screaming that this is a terrible idea, but I think I want to go for it."

"Are you absolutely sure?" Whoople asked.

"If it means I don't have to wade through an ocean of paperwork to get a job, I'm willing to give it a shot."

"I don't mean to pry, but what in Glob's name did paperwork do to garner such revulsion?"

"Maybe I'll tell you sometime, but you said yourself that we're keeping people waiting."

"*All right*," Whoople shrugged. "I don't know if this is the best idea, but if nothing else, it should be an interesting exercise in improvisation."

He turned back to the doorway, straightened himself out again, and took a deep breath.

"Follow my lead."

Chapter 4
The Interview

"Ladies, Gentlemen, and otherwise," Grand Master Whoople again addressed the walls as he and Alexander returned to the interview room. "Thank you once again for your patience. We apologize for the delay and are ready to resume the proceedings."

Once again, Alexander felt the sensation of hidden eyes trained on him. He *thought* he had been nervous before, but that was before he knew what they were really looking for.

"I must ask you all to forgive some apprehension on Alexander's part," Whoople continued. "He's new to the Federation, after all. With your express permission, I would like to hold off on any direct questions for now and carry on with the main article of performance."

With only a brief pause to acknowledge whatever he heard through his earpiece, the Grand Master turned to Alexander.

"We're ready to start," he said with a wink. "First things first, are you familiar with depuration tablets?"

"No, I don't think so."

"They're used for sanitation. Kind of complicated to explain quickly. Have you ever heard of nano swarms? Billions of microscopic nanobots able to act in unison?"

"I guess I've heard about that kind of thing on sci-fi shows."

"Well, you can imagine the depuration tablet acting like a nano swarm designed to cover your skin and keep it clean. It actually works completely differently, but it's a lot simpler to visualize that. Does a good job of sanitation and means we don't have to worry about showers."

"All right."

"This particular variety is also specially formulated to provide on-demand lubrication to certain areas."

"Sounds convenient," Alexander said, hoping his embarrassment wasn't showing as much as it felt like it was.

"It is! The downside is that it can get embedded in your clothes when you first apply it and having a conspicuously clean, slippery patch on your shirt can be a bit awkward. So, everything on you has to come off. My depuration's still good for another few weeks, but I can strip at the same time if that'd be more comfortable for you."

"Ah, yeah, sure," Alexander said, not sure it would.

Whoople began pulling off his shirt, and Alexander followed suit. He couldn't shake the notion that he was being watched since he *was*, but the fact that Whoople was the only one present in the room did make things a little easier. Momentarily distracted with taking off his own clothes, Alexander glanced up to see that the Grand Master had already disrobed and was briefly folding up his garments with his back turned to him.

Gawking slightly, Alexander glanced the alien over while taking off his pants. Whoople's dark purple-grey skin was devoid of any hair and mostly smooth, though there were plenty of odd ridges and lines that sharply defined his physical features. He wasn't ludicrously muscle-bound, but all the same, he was nicely toned. As the Grand Master bent over to set down his clothes, Alexander couldn't help but bring his gaze down to the alien's lower half.

'Damn,' Alexander thought. 'Proportions are a little weird, but not a half bad ███ {PUMPKIN PATCH}.'

It was only now that Alexander took the time to observe that Whoople stood on his toes, like what you'd see on the hind legs of a cat or dog. This revelation was quickly overshadowed as the Grand Master turned to face him once again. To his credit, Alexander tried his best *not* to immediately stare down at Whoople's crotch. However, the startling aspect that involuntarily drew his eye downward was that, in contrast to pretty much every other part of him, Whoople's ████ {WOO-HOO} was tinted a bright, cobalt blue that almost seemed to glow.

Not wanting to gawk, Alexander quickly turned away and heaped his clothes on the couch. Nervously checking himself over, he noted that his heart rate had jumped slightly. He felt a little annoyed with himself. It's not like this was his first time or anything, but it had been a number of years since college, and this was certainly much stranger circumstances than anything he'd gotten himself into even back then.

"Of all the things I should have been practicing..." Alexander mumbled to himself.

"Doing all right, Alexander?" the Grand Master asked.

"Uh, yes! I'm doing fine," he replied, trying not to stare at Whoople's bright blue ████ {WOODPECKER}.

"They can't hear what we're saying unless I activate the mic," Whoople assured him. "You don't need to worry about sounding like an amateur, at least. Just take a breath and keep calm."

"Right, okay."

"Come over, and I'll show you how to use the depuration tablet."

The Grand Master beckoned him over and handed him something that looked like one of those chewable tablets for heartburn but with a little bubble set in on one side.

"When you're ready, hold the tablet in the palm of your hand and break open the little popper on top. It should be pretty apparent when it starts working."

"Have these been tested on humans before?" Alexander asked cautiously.

"Yes. I've seen the trial period results, and this formulation is listed as perfectly safe. It's almost unheard of for depuration tablets to go bad. Although, if someone ever gives you one that's colored green with a red popper, *don't* use it without making sure that it's *definitely not* an Ewgruppian algae bath tablet. I cannot stress how much of a pain in the narbles it is to suddenly have a million eukaryotic organisms stuck up every nook and cranny."

"Ugh!" Alexander made a face.

"It's terrible, but don't worry. This tablet is fine."

Alexander took a deep breath and burst the popper with his thumb. The tablet broke into a few large pieces that immediately seemed to dissolve into his hand. He couldn't see anything happening, but he felt something ripple and spread like a wave across his skin. This fluid feeling went all the way up his arm and spread out across his chest like he was diving into a pool of water. As the sensation rushed up his neck, he was briefly caught with panic as it seemed poised to shoot straight into his mouth and down his throat. However, at the last second, the sensation mercifully halted right around his lips, nostrils, and eyelids. Alexander did squirm a little as it wormed its way a bit further down into his ears than he would have liked, but even there, it petered out before it got too deep.

Alexander had just enough time to adjust to this slight discomfort around his face when his attention switched to the depuration's progress down his waist. To his dismay, the rippling wave had no qualms about going right up his ▮▮▮ {ARTICHOKE}. He tensed up involuntarily as it washed over his ▮▮▮▮ {EGGPLANTS} and trickled down to his legs and feet. It took a second, but once it had finished maxing out its coverage, it wasn't so bad. Alexander's skin now felt soft and smooth, like he had just finished drying off after a nice shower.

"Wow," he said. "That wave is something to get used to, but once it's on, it feels pretty nice."

"Doesn't it? That should last you for a couple weeks. You'll still need a shower if you go tromping through mud, and you should always wash your hands as normal, but it does a darn good job at maintaining a higher level of cleanliness and sanitation than you'd get naturally."

"Cool."

"Are you comfortable with doing a quick turnaround to get a good look at you?"

"Uh, yeah. Sure."

Not entirely sure how to handle himself, Alexander did a little walk in a circle with his arms slightly raised. Whoople briefly flashed an involuntary smile as a veteran professional watching a novice at work. Alexander gave an embarrassed little shrug.

"That's fine," Whoople assured him. "Listen, Alexander, I don't mean to belittle you, but you look a little tense and nervous to me right now."

"No, that's fair," Alexander took a breath. "It's just... Well, this is a weird approach to sex for me. I had a few flings back in college, but those were just for fun."

"You don't need to worry so much. This is *supposed* to be the fun part of the job, after all. Here, sit down for a second."

The Grand Master walked over and respectfully guided him onto the low couch. Kneeling down beside him, Whoople glanced him over.

"Let's get you in the right place."

"What are you-?"

The question was cut off by the alien bending over and sticking out his ludicrously long tongue. Alexander was startled by its length and the fact that only a short way down from the deceptively dark tip, it took on the same bright cobalt blue as his ██████ {CRE-DENTIALS}. Without giving Smig any time to question or react, the Grand Master ran the entire length of his tongue across Alexander's █████ {AMBASSADOR} in a slow, rolling flick. He did this one more time as Alexander reflexively shifted and gripped the couch before coming back down and taking the whole █████ {RODEO} into his mouth in a quick dive. Alexander's reflexes flinched a little as the Grand Master's sharp teeth brushed against his █████ {PICKLE}, but the alien was clearly a professional who knew what he was doing. Going down as far as he could, Whoople buried his nose into Alexander's lower abdomen and swallowed around his ████ {CONDIMENT BOTTLE}.

"H-holy shit," Alexander gasped, wholly unprepared.

Whoople smirked. While still holding Alexander in his mouth, he coiled his tongue around his ██████ {WINGDOODLE} and slowly began stroking it while still sucking away. Alexander squirmed. He couldn't recall ever having a more intense ███████ *{CARNIVAL RIDE}*.

"Whoople I- I'm not going to, ah, last long if you keep thahh-that up," Alexander warned.

The Grand Master's tongue unraveled itself, and he released his hold on Alexander's ████ *{POPSICLE}*.

"Sorry, Alexander. Even Grand Masters can get carried away. This is my first time with an Earthling, and I have to say you don't taste too bad."

"Uh, thanks?" Alexander panted.

"Just to check, is that all normal for you?" he asked, pointing southward.

Alexander glanced down at his throbbing ██████ *{POOL NOODLE}*, which was now as hard as a rock.

"Yeah, that's what I've got."

"Perfect. Plenty to work with. Are you in a better mood to perform?"

"Well, it's still a weird situation, but I think I'm as ready as I'll ever be."

"I can keep going if you'd like," the Grand Master grinned.

Alexander's eyebrows screwed up in confusion.

"Um, I don't know. Don't get me wrong, that was the best █████ *{SAFARI}* I've ever had in my entire life, but it doesn't make much sense to me if you're doing all the, uh... *work* in the interview."

"There's no accounting for taste," Whoople shrugged. "I've been a Grand Master for almost 782 yelaageroos, intimately familiar with techniques and positions from across the entire multiverse, some of which can only be performed with my exceptionally rare-occurring prehensile █████ *{ANACONDA}*, yet even I'm still amazed by how often I come across people who enjoy getting *me* off and not expecting anything in return."

"Wow."

"Of course, there are also folks who like to hang upside down and read Aristotle while you sit with your legs wrapped around them and use your feet to knit tea cozies behind their back. But that's pretty rare, all things considered.."

"I see," Alexander said, wondering if he should ask how anyone in the Federation would know about Aristotle.

"Point is, Alexander, nobody wants you to try and do anything you aren't comfortable with. From what I've read on Earthlings, I figured that would make for a decent warm-up, but I'm not here to have you play outside of your league. Like I said before, the only incentive to do more than a bare minimum is to show the clients that you're capable of a wider variety of interactions, which means a larger pool of clients might take an interest, which in turn means a wider choice of contracts for you to pick from. Does that make sense?"

"Yeah, I can go along with that."

"So, what do you think? What are you up for here and now?"

"Well, I think I should show that I can do more than get ▉▉▉▉▉ ▉▉▉ {COMPENSATION}."

"All right," Whoople chuckled. "Would you like to take a more active role?"

"Yes," Alexander said somewhat hesitantly. "Um, I wanted to mention... don't take this the wrong way, but I've only ever been with girls before."

"It's a little late for me to run to the discombobulator and swap genders."

"You can do that?" Alexander asked incredulously.

"Grand Masters have to be flexible," Whoople smiled.

"Wow, okay... Ask about that another time, I guess. I mean, I don't have any problem with you being a guy. I just wanted you to know that this is unfamiliar territory for me."

"That's alright, Alexander. There's a first time for everything. Why don't we do something that crosses both circles of the Venn diagram? Ever done someone up the ▉▉▉▉ {APRICOT} before?"

"Once or twice," Alexander admitted.

"Well then, that shouldn't be too far outside your comfort zone, right?"

The Grand Master twisted around and planted his hands on the couch next to Alexander. His tail did a long slow flick from one side to the other as he got up on his knees and presented his sexy ███ {*MOON*}.

"Don't be afraid to make a show of things," Whoople said. "Do a little foreplay. Looks good and buys a little time to plan out your moves."

"Okay."

Alexander shuffled around onto his knees. Reaching out, he ran his hands down Whoople's lower back. The alien's skin was soft and very human-like, but something about it also reminded Alexander of the one time he got to pet a giant python at the zoo. Not slippery or even scaly, but very smooth.

"You, uh. You said the depuration stuff also acted like a lubricant?" he asked.

"Yep. It's automatic and context-sensitive in the spots where you'd expect, so just go for it, and it'll work itself out."

"All right."

Alexander made some circular, massaging motions around Whoople's back, gradually going lower and lower until he felt up his ████ {*GARBANZOS*}. Gracefully, the Grand Master swept one leg straight to spread out his ██████ {*SAND BAGS*}. Alexander suddenly stopped.

"You've got two ████████ {*FIRE ESCAPES*} back here," Alexander observed.

"Oh yeah, I do. Earthing males only have the one, don't they?"

"Yeah."

This revelation reminded Alexander of the nipples question, which made slightly better sense now than it had over the phone. Now, of course, his attention was grabbed by the fact that he hadn't noticed how many nipples the Grand Master sported, and the alien's chest was out of view. Under any other circumstances, he wouldn't have cared less, but now a pestering curiosity had been sparked in his brain. He tried rather unsuccessfully to put it out of his mind.

"So, uh. Does it... you know, *matter* which one?" Alexander asked.

"Nope! Pick whichever takes your fancy!"

"Okay then."

Alexander mentally shrugged and figured there wasn't any going back now. If there was one thing he'd learned from college, it was that a little exploration was a good idea before he even thought about putting his most sensitive parts forward. He slid his hand down the exposed crevice of Whoople's ▌▌▌▌ {KABUMPER} and circled his thumb around the Grand Master's topmost ▌▌▌▌ {MANHOLE COVER}. It didn't take much stimulation around this area for Alexander to notice a distinct sensation, which he took to be the lubrication effect. He was glad to find that it wasn't unpleasantly slick or oily, just nice and smooth. Emboldened by this relaxed resistance, Alexander pressed a finger in.

Whoople hummed agreeably as Alexander explored around a little. The lubrication effect was a little unusual, but aside from that, the experience wasn't anything out of the ordinary. More out of curiosity than anything, Alexander decided to test the bottom ▌▌▌▌ {TRAIN DEPOT} with his other hand, gently sliding another finger in. The Grand Master purred as he did some half massaging, half exploratory motions in and out with his fingers. Whoople stirred and slowly wiggled his hips a little, pressing back into Alexander's hands to increase the sensation.

"That all right?" Alexander asked.

"That's fine," the alien laughed. "Don't worry too much about me. I can take just about anything you could throw at me."

Whoople probably didn't quite mean for that to sound like a challenge, but Alexander was slowly slipping more into the swing of things, and it certainly echoed in his ear with a provocative ring. Removing his fingers, Alexander repositioned himself, scooching up between Whoople's legs.

"Well then, how about I throw something a little bigger at you?"

Something inside him groaned a little at using such a cheesy line, but Alexander couldn't back down now. As he repositioned himself, the Grand Master bent his knees a little, attempting to mitigate the height mismatch. Alexander ran his hands along the alien's ▌▌▌▌▌ {MACHICOLATIONS} and guided his ▌▌▌▌ {BRATWURST} up against Whoople's ▌▌▌▌▌ {BURGER BUNS}. The lubrication effect made everything silky smooth, and Alexander spent a few teasing moments rubbing himself between the alien's ██████ {PROMENADE}.

Leaning forward, he slid his hands up and around Whoople's chest. The Grand Master purred again as Alexander felt him out. Blindly exploring with his hands, Alexander found himself unconsciously searching for the alien's nipples. Curiously, as far as he could tell, the lanky interviewer didn't appear to have any that he could feel. Distracted by this apparent oddity, Alexander continued to fumble around as casually as he could. Not having any real view of what he was doing made it an interesting experience. As his hands explored further downward, he realized that Whoople also seemed to lack an apparent belly button.

Alexander was starting to think that his powers of observation were far too quickly distracted by brightly colored reproductive organs when his hands accidentally bumped into the Grand Master's █████ {PEPPERMINT STICK}. Whoople jumped ever so slightly, causing the equally startled Alexander to try and smooth the motion out. He hadn't intended to get down to this level, but now he found himself running his fingers down Whoople's ██████ {BATON}. The Grand Master's ██████ {MAYPOLE} was almost as soft as the rest of his skin, but it felt more taught, almost muscular. There was a bit of a ridge right at the base where it connected to the rest of his body, but then after that, Alexander noted a distinct lack of ████████ {SHOPPING BAGS}.

'Okay, brain,' he thought to himself. 'Let's quit trying to work out alien physiology by braille and get this over with.'

Wrapping his fingers around Whoople's ████ {DOODLE-BUG}, Alexander started ██████ {APPLYING THE HAND BRAKE} with a few slow motions to get a feel for things. The Grand Master gave a little sigh, enjoying the action. Relieved that he hadn't brought things to a halt at the very least, Alexander stuck to this for a bit, resuming his own movement between Whoople's ██████ {GRASSY KNOLL}. The general awkwardness of the situation gradually subsided as Alexander started to work himself up. It was also pretty obvious that the Grand Master was getting worked up, too, as his prehensile █████ {SERGEANT} had started to twist and writhe in impossible ways that made Alexander feel like he was trying to ███ ███ *{TICKLE}* an octopus tentacle.

Whoople sighed and wriggled pleasurably in his grip, and Alexander decided it was high time to do a little more for himself. Pulling back a little, Alexander kept up the action with one hand while using his other to guide his ████ *{FUN GUN}* down to Whoople's ██████ *{INNER SANCTUM}*. There was some initial resistance before the lubrication effect ramped up and allowed him to slide in. The ██████ *{INTERIOR}* of the alien's ███ *{POSTERIOR}* was warm and tight. The Grand Master arched his back and pushed into Alexander to drive him all the way home. Alexander squirmed a little as he felt Whoople flex beneath him. The Grand Master contracted the walls of his ██████ *{SUBWAY}*, rippling them up in a wave that was almost as intense as his ███████ *{SMOOCHES}* had been. Alexander grunted as his ████ *{HAMMER HANDLE}* was practically swallowed right up to the hilt. Now buried as deep as possible in Whoople's ████ *{SUMMER HOME}*, he rested himself against the Grand Master's back.

"Doing all right?" Whoople asked, peeking out from under an arm.

"Yeah," Alexander said, drawing it out in a sigh.

"Good!" The Grand Master flashed a mischievous little grin. "That *is* a little bigger than your fingers."

Alexander frowned a little. Pulling out of the alien's grasp, he ██████ *{RAMMED THE PROW}* with enough force to audibly slap against the Grand Master's █████ *{MELON}*. Whoople's ears flinched up a little in surprise as an emboldened Alexander began to █████ *{GO SPELUNKING}* in and out of him in earnest. Gamely, the alien challenged him by performing his massaging waves in time with Smig's ███████ *{FELICITATIONS}*. Alexander countered by upping the tempo on his reach-around, gripping Whoople's █████ *{JOYSTICK}* with both hands.

Both of them were breathing heavily now as they ███████ *{BURIED THE WEASEL}* against each other. Any concerns about hidden eyes were utterly forgotten as Alexander felt his ████ *{EXCITEMENT}* building. He was determined to hold on for as long as possible, but Whoople's ▆▆▆▆ *{BIVOUACKING}* was effortlessly keeping pace with Alexander's ▆▆▆▆▆▆▆ *{FORBIDDEN POLKA}*. Hoping to catch the Grand Master by surprise, Alexander suddenly pulled fully out of Whoople's lower ▆▆▆▆▆▆▆ *{HAPPY PLACE}*, only to immediately ▆▆▆▆ *{BURGLARIZE}* the ▆▆▆▆ *{CHAMBER OF MYSTERIES}* directly above.

Alexander was rewarded with an adorable little chirrup noise from the startled alien. Hoping to maintain his slim lead, he quickly picked up his pace. Whoople squirmed underneath him, trying to squeeze Alexander again, but the Grand Master had lost his rhythm. The alien's bright blue ▆▆▆▆ *{COCKTAIL}* waggled side to side, but Alexander kept his grip on it, twisting his strokes in unusual ways as they ▆▆▆▆▆▆ *{BASTED THE TURKEY}*. Even with the upper hand, Alexander knew he was building up fast, and ▆▆▆▆▆▆ *{GAVE IT THE BEANS}* hard to try and take the Grand Master over the edge before he reached it himself.

A crazy idea popped into Alexander's head. It wasn't necessarily a good idea, but there wasn't time to reason things out. Maneuvering around, he slid his other hand down the base of Whoople's ▆▆▆▆ *{DACHSHUND}*, between his legs, and back up to reach the alien's unoccupied ▆▆▆▆ *{PORTCULLIS}*. It was a bit of a contortion act, but Alexander found he could get a finger or two hooked in without getting in the way of everything else. The Grand Master moaned in earnest as Alexander ▆▆▆▆▆ *{PLAYED PEEK-A-BOO}* with all the good spots on his bottom half at once.

The Grand Master twisted again and clutched the couch in front of him with whitened knuckles. Alexander was desperately trying to keep up the pace, focusing on three separate actions simultaneously, but he could feel himself being driven to the breaking point. Right as Alexander felt like he was going to explode, Whoople made a high-pitched little squeak and tensed up underneath him. The Grand Master ▆▆▆▆▆▆▆ *{CAPITULATED}* in a jolting fashion against Smig's hand as a streak of white shot out onto the couch in front of them. Whoople finally let out with an unmistakable cry of ▆▆▆▆▆ *{HOBBLEDEHOY}*. He tensed up again and again as several successive shots painted the upholstery.

This had distracted Alexander for a moment, but the Grand Master's ██████ {EXCELSIOR} had clamped down hard on his ████ {BROOM HANDLE} and maxed out his own sensations. He finally reached the edge and buried himself deep in a final thrust, ████████ {CATAPULTING} his ████ {SALVO} into the Grand Master's ████ {BULKHEAD} with his own involuntary cry. Alexander didn't have nearly as much to give as Whoople, but he was still ███████ {POUNDING PAVEMENT} as the alien started to wind down. As the Grand Master's death grip on Smig's █████ {HORNSWOGGLE} relaxed, Alexander slipped out. Both of them flinched reflexively as they disentangled themselves. Twisting around and flopping back onto the couch, they sat for a while to catch their breath. Whoople was the first to turn to Alexander.

"Now that was an interview!" the Grand Master said with a satisfied grin.

{EDITORIAL NOTE: Due to some rather cheeky and borderline inappropriate insertions on the part of Sir Hucklebourn, the upper echelon of B.A.S.T.A.R.D.S. has had him sacked. The remainder of the redactions in this book shall be provided by Lord Mipper-Hum-Bailicorn. We apologize for any inconvenience.}

Chapter 5
The Audience

Things moved quickly after the interview. Alexander could barely recall the sparse smattering of questions he had answered before being ushered back to the dressing room. He had collapsed on a chair for a brief minute to catch his breath and was just starting to put his pants back on when a very excited Whoople burst in with a stack of papers.

"Alexander! You've got a big one!" the Grand Master exclaimed. "No, not just a big one, the *biggest* one! You've got a contract offer from Chancellor Bulbeeyoog!"

Alexander looked at him like a cow looks at an oncoming train.

"That's... good?" he asked.

"It's unbelievably good!" Whoople said. "Chancellor Bulbeeyoog is the leader of the entire Federation of Everything! Nobody in the entire multiverse could offer you a better deal. I've looked over the contract, and if you quit after even just a weekend, you'd still be eligible for separation pay and a retirement fund bigger than most planetary GDPs combined!"

"Are you serious?"

"You better believe it, Alexander. I tried calculating the odds, and now my calculator is screaming. I've never had one do that before, and I don't know how to get it to stop, but that's something to deal with later. This may not have been what you were going for, but you lucked out big time."

"This is legit?"

"No joking, Alexander. This is legit."

"Wow," Alexander blinked. "I don't know what to say. I, uh, I don't know anything about this Chancellor guy. What's he like?"

"Well, nobody knows for sure. He's got a hell of a reputation in politics, but his personal life is almost a complete mystery. Pretty much everything connected to him is a government secret. They even blur out his face in all of his public appearances. I didn't even know he was one of the viewing clients until the offer came in. Let's see, here's a picture of him."

Whoople held up a laminated page with an official-looking, half-length portrait of a vast, dragon-like figure wearing what appeared to be an eight-piece suit, which seemed excessive until you accounted for all of the odd accouterments the alien was endowed with; scales, claws, tail, and the like. True to form, the figure's head was pixelated out, though Alexander's attention was focused more on the outline of an average-sized Earthling that had been juxtaposed next to the Chancellor to provide a size comparison.

"He seems a lot bigger than I anticipated," Alexander said.

"I can hardly believe it myself. Out of all the people in the multiverse, you wind up scoring the head honcho of head honchos."

"Well, yeah, but I mean physically. He looks huge."

"What? Oh, yeah. He is kinda big, isn't he?" Whoople turned the sheet around to stare at it. "Well, clearly, he thinks he can make something work. Maybe they've finally made progress on that enbiggenator they keep talking about, but let's not get bogged down. This is a once-in-a-lifetime event that could get you set up for all eternity, or the heat death of the universe, whichever comes first. The thing here is that if you want it, you need to accept it very quickly. Offers of employment for the Chancellor's private retinue are Federally mandated to last only for a very brief period of time before they expire. Lots of political and security concerns wrapped up in that."

"How long do I have to think it over?"

"Wait a minute," Whoople said.

The Grand Master briefly ducked back into the side room. This time Alexander noticed the sound of Whoople's calculator continuing its unceasing, breathless scream. The alien quickly returned, closing the door and muffling the small machine's torment.

"About fifteen-ish minutes," Whoople replied. "I hope I can get that poor thing reset at some poin-"

"What?!" Alexander's eyes boggled a little. "Really? Is that enough time to even read through a contract?"

"I've already read it thoroughly, Alexander, and speaking as someone who's read and negotiated contracts for the last 800 ye-laageroos, I can say without a doubt that the deal you're getting is more than fair. I know it's a big decision, but that doesn't mean it can't be an easy one. Even if you somehow regret your decision later, the Chancellor's contract has practically zero lifetime or non-negotiable obligations. You can walk away just about any old time you want."

"Well... sounds like it'd be pretty dumb for me to say no."

"You'll do it?"

"Screw it. Why not?"

"Fantastic! Grab your things and follow me!"

Alexander only had enough time to grab the rest of his clothes from off the floor before chasing after Whoople as the Grand Master strode hurriedly out into the halls. The alien's long-legged stride looked like a brisk walk, but Alexander had to jog to catch up. It was quite tricky to keep up speed while pulling on his shirt, and he opted to go barefoot so he didn't risk losing track of the Grand Master and getting lost in the gargantuan ship. It wasn't long, though, before Whoople slowed down and gestured him into a waiting room.

"Have a seat Alexander," the Grand Master said as he strode up to the counter. "I'll get you set up."

At first, Alexander thought it was the same place where he had entered the ship, but he soon realized that the layout of this one was flipped around like a mirror image. The secretary at the desk even had her eyeballs on the opposite side of her face. Smig sat down and took the opportunity to pull on his socks and shoes while Whoople talked excitedly with the secretary. After only a brief chat, he turned and called out.

"All right, you're hired!"

"Great!" Alexander replied as the alien came over to him.

"I still can't believe it. I got someone hired for the Chancellor of the Federation! Here, take this and hold onto it. This is a temporary employee ID you can use to identify yourself until your info gets populated across the automated Federal system."

He handed Alexander a laminated card, featuring an animated version of his head spinning around that still somehow managed to show Smig in the most unflattering manner possible at every angle.

"Now listen, son," Whoople continued. "The Chancellor himself wants to have a brief word with you directly via telepholographic projection. He's not going to be in the same room, of course, but it's going to feel like he is. I don't want to make you uneasy, Alexander, but this is an exceptional occurrence, and I want to emphasize that you're not merely meeting with your employer. You are having a direct audience with the most powerful individual next to Globbo himself."

At the mention of whoever this Globbo character was, the Grand Master made some kind of motion with one hand that was oddly reminiscent of a sign of the cross.

"We don't have enough time to go over proper protocol, so just be courteous and if you remember nothing else, avoid speaking about his extended familial relations at all costs! From what I've heard, a lifetime sentence in the Federal Dungeons would be a far happier fate than what befalls those who raise that topic with the Chancellor."

"Oo-oh," Alexander replied, fully taken in by Whoople's deadly serious tone.

"Of course, they could just be rumors!" the Grand Master exclaimed. "Either way, *I* certainly wouldn't chance it. Just don't speak out of turn and I'm sure you'll do fine!"

The alien gave Smig a pat on the shoulder and headed for the door.

"Give me a ring if you need," he called out. "Their resource manager should take good care of you, but as your agent, I'm always available for advice."

"Uh... thanks, Whoople," Alexander replied, not entirely recovered from the tonal whiplash of the Grand Master's parting words.

"Don't mention it, Alexander! I'd have never thought that I'd get someone hired by the Chancellor. They're never going to believe this at choir practice."

And with that, the Grand Master disappeared into the hallway. After only a short pause, the secretary at the desk bent over towards her desk.

"Beeeeep," she chimed, this time without even the aid of an actual intercom. "Mr. Alexander Smig, please come to the counter."

Smig shook his head and walked up to the desk.

"Hello, Mr. Smig!" the secretary greeted him cheerfully. "The Chancellor would like to have a brief Telepholographic conference in order to meet you. If you are ready, please step through the door on your right. An aide will be present to get you situated."

"Okay then," Alexander replied, wondering more than ever now what he'd gotten himself into. "Thanks, I guess."

"Thank you, Mr. Smig!" she merrily proclaimed, swiveling back to whatever hibernation mode these secretaries seemed to default to.

Alexander took a deep breath and walked through the door. Inside was something rather like a dark-colored conference room devoid of any chairs. Towards the far wall stood an immense, desk-like structure, taller than Smig himself, with a separate platform in front of it. Beside this stood a smartly dressed aide, who had clearly been anticipating Smig's ingress. At first glance, this alien didn't look too wildly different from an Earthling, save for the two tails that swept gracefully up behind him as he went. However, it was soon obvious that his arms and legs had no singularly defined joints but flexed freely like tentacles. Upon closer inspection, even his elaborately swirled strands of hair also appeared to be tentacles, partially obscuring a second mouth located smack dab in the middle of his forehead.

"Mon-sigg-noar Ahl-ecks-aan-dur?" the aide spoke from his forehead mouth with an extraordinarily thick accent.

"Uh... That's me?" Alexander answered dubiously.

"Gre-EE-tings Mon-sigg-noar! If the your to be of any-thing is in of nee-ding, give to mind of kee-ping the name is Gleeboh."

"Ah, your name is Gleeboh?"

The aide lingered in his pose, giving the subtle impression that his patience went stale at the drop of a hat.

"Yeees! Gleeboh is of the name to give in kee-ping," he replied in a slower and seemingly more condescending tone.

The aide's upper mouth had taken on that forced kind of smile that well-practiced customer service agents employ; however, his lower mouth (hidden somewhat by his wriggling mustache) gave hardly a tenth of the same effort. This was accentuated by his squinting eyes that tried only vaguely to suggest that he was cheerful and *not* regarding Smig with the same distaste that one typically reserves for a wad of chewing gum that has become stuck to the underside of a shoe.

"In the wait-ing of the room from the view-ing in Chancellor, plee-as to move in practize-ment the rostrum."

Alexander gathered more from Gleeboh's gesturing than his confusing speech pattern that he was being asked to stand on the platform in front of the giant desk. With some hesitation, he stepped up onto it, all the while eyeing the aide for uneasy confirmation. Thankfully Gleeboh seemed satisfied enough with what he was doing.

"The ade-quate of most is in move-ment!" he proclaimed in the same tone and manner in which you might congratulate a toddler. "Plee-as to your of kee-ping and of wait-ing to be in use!"

With whatever admonishment that was, Gleeboh turned and made to leave through another side door. Before he disappeared, the aide tapped a panel on the wall and spoke briefly into it.

"The broad's ready."

It happened so quickly and quietly that Smig almost didn't believe he had truly heard it. He swore that Gleeboh had just downright dropped his accent and demeanor for that brief second. Either way, he had no time to question it before the alien exited, and Alexander found himself alone. There was a long, silent pause as he glanced around, trying to tell if his mind was playing tricks on him.

After about a minute or two, just as he was starting to wonder what he was doing here, the lights dimmed slightly. This seemed to be a cue for things to start as music began to play from hidden speakers surrounding the room. The tune was odd and somewhat disjointed to Smig's ear, but it clearly had the character of a "Hail to the Chief" style anthem. Not entirely sure what to do, he decided to stand at attention.

He was a little startled when the platform beneath him began to rise upwards. The movement was slow and smooth, but Smig still braced himself a little from not expecting it. The lack of any rails around the edges didn't help ease his mind either. Gracefully, it glided to a stop when it came level with the top of the desk in front of him. The music 'blurped' with a final flourish and went silent.

"Federal citizens," a charismatic voice boomed from the speakers. "His esteemed excellency Bulbeeyoog, Chancellor of the Federation of Everything and Protector of its Citizen's Rights, Liberties, and Dental Benefits."

A humongous section of the back wall faded away to reveal a darkened hall. Two shimmering red rings were glowing in the black chamber, like massive brake lights in the rain. Out of the darkness emerged a figure larger than most of the equipment Smig had ever driven. The light revealed the Chancellor's immense suit, razor-sharp claws, and sweeping tail, but it did not fully reveal his face. This was still obscured by a pixelated effect exactly as it had appeared in his official photograph. Smig could roughly gauge the outline of the draconic alien's head, but even the red glowing light in his eyes had disappeared and couldn't be distinguished anymore.

Despite knowing this was a holographic whatever, Alexander still swore he could feel the ground vibrate under his feet as the Chancellor took a seat at the desk in front of him. The Chancellor sat calmly with his hands resting on the desk in front of him, yet the whole room was saturated with that heavy aura that seemed to radiate from exceptionally powerful individuals. Alexander could almost feel it dripping off the ceiling onto his head.

"Alexander Smig, I presume?" the Chancellor asked in a deep, rich voice.

The alien's tone wasn't menacing in any particular way, but anything coming from someone that was at least twice as tall as you and seemingly (if not literally) in a position to send you flying with a casual flick of the wrist couldn't help but seem at least a little ominous. Alexander squinted at the shimmering space where the alien's eyes probably were, growing steadily more uneasy as he couldn't even tell exactly where they *should* be.

"Yes! That's me, sir."

"Good to meet you, Alexander," Bulbeyoog said politely. "You'll have to excuse our first encounter being through projection. Even if my schedule wasn't so busy, we still have some security checks to clear before we can meet in person. The clearance process is a little intense, but I promise once it's over, things will go a lot smoother."

The Chancellor crossed one leg over the other and leaned back a little. Smig still couldn't quite believe the scale of the alien before him. He hoped that Bulbeeyoog's size was at least a little exaggerated by the projection because he couldn't even begin to contemplate what you would do to please someone with such gargantuan proportions.

"Would you mind if I asked a question, Alexander?" the Chancellor asked. "Nothing terribly important. Mainly just curious about something I've only seen on Earth, is all."

"Uh, sure," Smig replied. "Though, I'm not the most knowledgeable guy on the planet."

"That's all right. Do you know what is the purpose of a pergola?"

Smig was a little taken aback by the question.

"Uh, you mean like one of those big arbors with the slats you put over a patio or something?"

"Yes, exactly! What is the point of those? They don't exactly give you much shade, and they're no use at all if it rains."

"To be honest, sir, I have no idea. I guess people just like the look of them."

The Chancellor leaned back in his chair and arched his fingers together as if deep in thought.

"Mm, aesthetics," he murmured conspiratorially. "That's what everyone *seems* to think."

Silence reigned as the red light of Bulbeeyoog's eyes began to glow once again. Thin wisps of smoke escaped the shimmering pixelation of his face, leaving Alexander to stand in nervous silence at whatever dire contemplation was taking place. He nearly jumped when an intercom chime broke the ice.

"Beeeeep," toned the secretary. "Your 28 o'clock appointment is coming up, Mr. Chancellor."

"Thank you," Bulbeeyoog sighed. "I'm afraid we'll have to cut this short for now, Alexander. I look forward to meeting you in person."

The Chancellor rose from his seat and leaned over the desk. The dim glow of his eyes had not fully abated and smoldered above Smig's head like burning embers.

"A chaperone has been assigned to pick you up when you leave. I want you to know that there are some practices you might find unusual that we have for security reasons. I ask that you follow along with whatever is asked of you. This is as much for your safety as it is for mine."

"Yes, sir!" Alexander said.

He certainly wasn't going to complain with the Chancellor looming directly over him like that. Satisfied, the alien straightened up and turned to leave.

"As I said before, the clearance process will be rather arduous, but it shouldn't take long. As long as you have nothing to hide, Mr. Smig, we should see each other soon."

The Chancellor turned to fixate him one last time with his burning gaze.

"Though if you do have something to hide, you won't appreciate the circumstances when we do."

And with that, the draconic alien dissolved into nothing, leaving Alexander with only the strangest impression that he could even smell the smoke that had been rising from the Chancellor. Quietly, the platform returned him to the ground, and he somewhat shakily stepped off.

"What the hell have I gotten myself into," he thought to himself.

Chapter 6:
The Chaperone

Alexander emerged from the conference room, half wondering if it was too late to get out and catch a flight to Tasmania to hide with his Aunt. He had little time to contemplate the option when a door opened on the other side of the waiting room, revealing a short, green, blob-like alien with two arms, two legs, one eyeball on a stalk on top of its head, and a mustache that looked like an old mop head.

As it stepped out, it tripped and knocked a right mess of buckets, brooms, and spray bottles out onto the floor. Stumbling noisily for a moment, it hastily kicked the cleaning implements back into the small room it had come from and slammed the door on the impending avalanche. Straightening up and trying to regain some composure, the strange alien came forward and held up a clipboard.

"Alexander Smig?" It asked aloud.

"That's me," Alexander said.

"Aha! I am here to transport you to your destination *if you would so desire.*"

The alien blinked at him in an exaggerated manner. Alexander wasn't entirely sure what to make of this, but the same could be said for most every alien he'd encountered except possibly Grand Master Whoople. He glanced at the secretary for some kind of reassurance, but she seemed to be entirely preoccupied with what

Alexander could only assume was some kind of cosmetic ritual. She was dipping her elbows into some kind of waxy, pinkish substance and using a bizarre implement to trace little lines of the stuff down her arms in odd patterns.

"Uh... sounds good," Alexander replied, having decided he didn't want to stay here much longer in any case.

"Excellent!" the alien cried. "If you would be so kind as to follow me."

Alexander followed the odd fellow as the chaperone led him back out into the hall and walked briskly through the twisting corridors. Eventually, they emerged into a large docking bay filled with smaller ships that looked for all the world like a multilevel parking garage. The chaperone wandered up to a vessel that looked like the spaceship equivalent of a dilapidated Geo Metro and began to unlock the doors.

"Are we going to fly in that?" Alexander asked.

"Uh, yes!" the chaperone answered. "Yes, we are."

"I don't mean to be rude, but it looks a little run-down to me. Is this some kind of like, disguise, or something for security?"

"Disguise?" the chaperone asked, staring at the ship for a moment. "Uh... Yes! The appearance of the scooter *is* disguised for security reasons. How clever of you to notice! It's perfectly... *capable* of traveling in space. Please, take a seat."

"Okay..."

Alexander retained doubts about the vehicle, especially as it took a couple slams for the door to latch adequately. Buckled in, the chaperone slid into the driver's seat next to him and started the engine. It powered on pretty quick, which eased a little anxiety in Alexander's mind right until they pulled out of the parking spot by lifting straight up. The ship wobbled, and Alexander felt like he was on a roller coaster as the track was coming apart. He grabbed onto the only section of the dashboard that looked solid as they swooped around the docking bay.

"Whoa!" the chaperone exclaimed, quickly flipping some switches. "Silly me! I always forget to switch on the internal velocity smoothers before taking off. Give it a second to warm up."

The small ship continued to twist and tumble unpredictably. The chaperone glanced back and forth between the instrument panels for a moment before he leaned forward and gave the dashboard a hearty thwack with his fist. Several of the dial displays jumped around as an ominous 'clunk' noise came from somewhere underneath their seats. Gradually, the scooter's motion smoothed out, and the roller coaster feeling subsided, though it still reminded Alexander of a job a long time ago where he'd had to drive up and down some old streets in Spokane for a few months. They called it pothole city for a reason.

"There we go!" the chaperone said. "Don't worry, it always does that."

Zipping around and around the spiraling levels of the garage, they finally came to the main exit. The chaperone pulled up to a little booth to pay for the parking but spent a moment shuffling through some clutter on the floor before pulling out a screwdriver. This he jammed into the broken crank mechanism to wind the window down. After tossing a few plastic bills into the machine, he spent nearly a full minute laboriously winding the unwilling crank back to the up position before shooting out of the cruiser and into the vast, dark expanse of space. Alexander noted with some concern that the whistling sounds he'd heard around the door seals before were now silent in the vast vacuum of the cosmos. But he wasn't suffocating yet, so things were probably fine.

The craft flew on for a few minutes in awkward silence.

"So, uh, how long is the flight?" Alexander asked.

"Oh, not terribly long. Let me see."

The chaperone poked some buttons, and some numbers flickered up on a display screen in the middle.

"About 0.00744048 yelaageroos," he replied.

"I see. Is there, say, a conversion rate for that to some kind of Earth measurement?"

"Earth? Hmm."

A few more button presses garbled the numbers and popped up new ones.

"Looks like that's about 0.0002853882739726 years."

"Ah. Well, uh... thanks, I guess."

"No problem!"

Another awkward silence followed. Alexander couldn't tell if the uneasy feeling in his stomach was from the situation he had gotten himself into with the Chancellor or if it was the worryingly ramshackle appearance of his immediate surroundings. Either way, he was already toying with the potentially awkward idea of starting up a conversation with the weird chaperone when the alien cut short the consideration by starting it up themselves.

"So, you're a concubine, huh?" the green blob quipped.

"Uh, yeah," Smig replied without a lot of conviction.

"Funny, I wouldn't peg you for being the type. But I guess looks ain't everything!"

Alexander took a second to parse that as an insult.

"Excuse me?" he asked.

"I'm just yanking your chain," The alien grinned. "Glob knows I wouldn't be cut out for that kind of work. I mean, look at me! I look like a green kabump, for crying out loud! No, sir. I betcha could get in with just about anybody you asked for."

The chaperone leaned over and softly jabbed him with an elbow.

"Speaking of, can I ask if you're working for anyone in particular? Scouts honor, I'm not with any tabloids! Just curious."

"You mean you don't know?" Alexander asked. "It seems funny they wouldn't even tell you I'm working for the Chancellor."

"Uh, The Chancellor?" the chaperone asked quietly.

"Yeah, Chancellor Bull-something? I can't even pronou-"

"Chancellor Bulbeeyoog?" the alien blurted.

"Yeah, that's the one."

"Great cripes!" the chaperone exclaimed excitedly. "You're not the Chancellor's concubine, are you!?"

"Uh, well, I was just hired, but yeah."

"Holy shnipples! I just kidnapped a concubine from Chancellor Bulbeeyoog."

"You what!?"

"Listen, I thought you were just a concubine for some ordinary chump! If I'd have known you were in the Chancellor's retinue, I'd have at least put on a tie or slicked back my hair or something."

"You're *kidnapping* me?" Alexander asked incredulously.

"Well, duh! Wasn't it obvious? Don't tell me you actually fell for this number."

The chaperone peeled off his mustache, revealing that it had, in fact, been an old mop head the entire time. Smig stared at him.

"I mean... that does explain a few things, but I don't *want* to be kidnapped."

"Then why, for Glob's sake, did you come with me?"

"I don't know! I was supposed to get picked up by a chaperone, and you were right there and called for me by name!"

"Of course I said your name. It's on the publicly available Federal Employment Tertiary Checklist for Hiring and Internal Notary Gubbins. I did the standard Kidnapping Initiation Declaration and Notification of Abduction Procedure. I even winked at you in an exaggerated manner!"

Alexander looked at him in disbelief.

"*You only have one eye!* How am I supposed to tell the difference between a wink and a blink?"

"Oh, yeah. That's a fair point," the chaperone admitted as if he'd never considered it before. "But shouldn't the fact that I came out of a janitor's closet and the sketchy piece of- I mean the perfectly functional but clearly off-brand transportation scooter have rung any alarm bells in your head?"

"I don't know!"

"You just went along with it because I said your name," the alien squinted at him.

"Okay! Look, *pal.* Pretty much every single alien I've dealt with has been weird or crazy in some way or another. How am I supposed to determine what's out of the ordinary around here? Also, you knew I was a concubine, but you had no idea that I was hired by the Chancellor?"

"Your *name* and *job title* are F.E.T.C.H.I.N.G. Your *employer* is A.S.I.N.I.N.E. They're radically different lists, and I can't be bothered to read them all! Do you know how much trouble I could get into if the union catches wind that I picked up someone who apparently didn't want to be kidnapped?"

"Why would I *want* to be kidnapped!?" Alexander screamed in frustration.

The kidnapper turned and looked at him like he was nuts.

"Flipping palooza, kid. Are you new to the Federation or something?"

"Yes! I'd never even heard of the Federation until, like, a month ago!"

"What's a month?"

Alexander took a deep breath and ran his hands through his hair.

"Just give me one good reason why *anybody* would want to get kidnapped!"

"There are lots of reasons! I mean, it's none of my business what reason the client has, but people do it all the time to bail out of one mess or another. Like, maybe you're getting married to someone who's just too handsome for you to love, and you need an easy excuse for ditching the guy."

"Too handsome to love?" Alexander asked incredulously.

"Well, I don't know! That's what the ransom note for my fiancee said, at least! Personally, I think she has it in her head that I'm too stingy with my money. The note didn't even bother asking for cash. *Maybe* if they had thrown out an amount, I could have haggled with them a bit, and she could have seen that I care enough to do that, at least! Point is, if you don't have a good reason to be kidnapped, you shouldn't follow a professional kidnapper when he does his bit!"

Alexander stared at the kidnapper, completely at a loss for words.

"Jeez Louise!" the alien continued. "Now you've got both of us in a right pickle. For all intents and purposes, I've *stolen* a halfwit concubine. How the hoopla did a green amateur like you even land that job?"

"I don't know! I just did an interview, and the guy offered me a contract."

"What? Just like that? What kind of interview was this? Who interviewed you?"

"Grand Master Whoople!" Smig practically shouted.

The chaperone fell silent for a second.

"Ooohhh, that kind of interview," he said with revelation. "You seriously played pelvic pinochle with a Grand Master?"

"Why is that your first assumption?" Smig asked defensively.

"Good grief, kid. Grand Masters are only called in to do one of two things, and no offense, but your feet don't look nearly dexterous enough to knit tea cozies."

Alexander glanced down at his shoes and back at the kidnapper.

"Okay, so I did the other thing." he admitted.

"Did you bribe him to make it look good?" the alien asked with an unwelcome poke of his elbow.

"What? No!"

"Well, you must have done something truly remarkable then. Grand Masters are notoriously difficult to impress. About the only thing I know of that would spike on their radar is going at 'em and getting them to orgasm before you do, but that's darn near impossible!"

Smig turned away reflexively. He couldn't figure out how this train wreck of a conversation was so stacked against him, but he was too upset and embarrassed to think clearly. The kidnapper stared at him again.

"You didn't, did you?"

"Look, he didn't make a big deal out of it," Alexander began. "I just-"

"Whaaat!" the kidnapper's eye bugged out of his head. "You got a Grand tootin' Master to hit the big O before you? Are you serious?"

"This isn't what I want to talk about!" Smig said, trying to keep it together.

"Is this a prank? Are there hidden cameras somewhere?"

"How the hell would I know if there are cameras? It's *your* car!"

"Did you *really* get hired by the Chancellor?" the chaperone squinted at him. "How do I know for sure you aren't just trying to pull a fast one on me for a free kidnapping?"

"A free kidnap-" Alexander nearly lost it. "No! Look, I've got an employee ID card right here with Bulbee-whatsit's name on it as my emplo- why does it say 'BIMBO' under job title?"

"Bilateral Inter-Marital Bipedal Orderly," the kidnapper explained. "One of those weird, archaic classifications that's been in use for millions of yelaageroos. Lemme have a gander at that for a second, would ya?"

The kidnapper pulled out a corded scanner that looked for all the world like it had been pulled out of a supermarket from the 1970s and scanned Smig's card. The center console made several whirring noises before bringing up the pixelated photo of Chancellor Bulbeeyoog with a ping!

"GREAT CRIPES!" the kidnapper nearly jumped out of his seat. "You weren't kidding! You genuinely are working for the Chancellor!"

"I told you!" Alexander said.

"So let me get this straight, you were just hired by him and were supposed to be escorted somewhere, but instead, you took off with me because I used your name, and you didn't know any better."

"Yeah, and for the record, he had just finished explaining to me that they do unusual things for security reasons, so I thought your whole routine was just because of that!"

"He said?" the alien asked. "Did you actually *talk* to the Chancellor of the Federation?"

"I mean, it was one of those hologram things, but yeah, I talked to him."

The kidnapper was suddenly looking a much paler shade of green.

"Oh great Globbo," he said quietly. "We might be in a whole world of trouble."

"What's this 'we' stuff? I didn't ask to be kidnapped by a giant pistachio!"

"Well, hey! Frankly, I'm as upset as you are. But I can't exactly go waltzing you right back to the employment agency saying 'Oh, he didn't want to be kidnapped.' and expect to come out of that in one piece."

"Can't you just drop me off, and I can explain it was an honest mistake?"

"Oh, no. They've got the plate number for my scooter and a copy of my kidnapping license. Even if you *do* tell the truth, there's no guarantee that they'll believe you, and I could get into *serious* trouble for this. Under normal circumstances, I could arrange for you to have a dramatic escape from captivity. You know, like if you changed your mind and decided to marry the guy despite his dashing good looks. But let's consider for a moment the fact that the person noting your sudden and conspicuous absence is the flipping *Chancellor* of the gall-dang *Federation of Everything*."

"My absence against my will."

"Yes, against your will. Listen, you don't seem like a suicidal type, so I think it's prudent to point out that, willing or no, the ultimate head of the entire known multiverse hired you to one of the highest and most personal of positions that he can bestow, and you didn't show up. Not only did you *not* show up, you jumped ship right as soon as you got the job. Now imagine trying to explain that to the supreme minister of ministers in a way that doesn't sound sketchy as all get out. You think he'd seriously buy a story like that?"

"Whoople said nobody knows what he's really like."

"Well, yeah. Nobody's sure, but we're talking about the emperor of politicians! Do you want to take the chance that he's clawed his way to the top of the biggest pile short of becoming some sort of deity, but in reality, he's a nice, soft sweetheart brimming with forgiveness and understanding? You even talked to him! Did he look that way to you?"

Alexander recalled the draconic figure looming over his head. The scent of something burning and the shimmering red glow etched itself in his mind's eye.

"... I guess not."

"Take it from me; keeping away from him is almost certainly the *safest* option at this point."

"How are we supposed to avoid the most powerful person in the universe?"

"Well, in theory, it's easier than you might think. Space is big, and there's more bureaucracy between us and him than you could shake a stick at. Why, short of randomly bumping straight smack into his cruiser out in the middle of deep space, there's next to no chance of him physically finding us while we're scooting around."

A collosal thump rocked the little scooter, knocking both of them sideways.

"Holy moly!" the kidnapper exclaimed.

"What happened? What did we hit?" Alexander scrambled, staring wildly out the windows to see what had hit them.

"Oh, relax, kid, it was just a small meteoroid. How funny would that have been if that was the Chancellor's cruiser right then?"

"God. Not funny at all."

"Oh, lighten up. Tell you what, let's find a spot to land and think for a minute. I'm working on some ideas that might develop into plans, and I shouldn't get too distracted from flying right now."

"Yeah, I guess I'd rather not top off this whole fiasco with dying in space."

The craft flew on in silence for a terse moment. Alexander buried his head in his hands and wondered where everything went wrong.

"So, mister optimism," the alien piped up. "You got a name?"

Smig stared at him incredulously.

"Are you this thick all the time or does it take practice?" he asked.

"Oh, it takes lots of practice."

"Yes, I have a name. You *used* it to lure me into this death trap. Remember?"

"Oh yeah. Alexander Smig, was it?"

"Yes!"

"Got it!"

The kidnapper returned to flying the scooter and eventually began quietly humming to himself. It was cheerful in that maddening sort of way that forced Alexander to decide between strangling him and potentially dying alone in space or talking to him again. It was a close call, but talking narrowly won out.

"So, do you have a name?" he asked abruptly.

"Hmm? Oh, certainly! One moment."

The kidnapper pushed a button on the dashboard. The screen flickered again and whirled like a slot machine for a few seconds before coming to a stop at a name. The kidnapper squinted hard and read it aloud.

"The name's Ryan... uh... Ryan Sss-chuh-meh-did-Tt-Kee?"

"Ryan Schmidtke?" Smig read.

The alien looked at Alexander.

"Is that how you pronounce that? Schmidtke?"

"I think so."

"All right. Well, that's my name!"

"I *see*. And is that your real name?" Alexander asked sarcastically

"Oh, for land's sake, what part of 'professional kidnapper' is so hard to understand? I had to get my real name removed when I took the job. You can't risk having one of those in my line of work. I have one generated for all of my customers."

"Huh, is that a common thing to do?"

"No, outside of kidnapping, most people stick with their real names. That's why most of them are so weird and unpronounceable."

"Riiight."

Chapter 7
The Contract

"So, Ryan," Alexander asked. "Where exactly are we going?"

"Well, I've got a hidey-hole not too far from here. It's pretty standard as far as kidnapper bases are. Just a little stopover spot with a cheap-ish motel and a diner across the street."

"Ah," Alexander frowned. "I just thought of something. If this kidnapping is supposed to be a 'service.' am I supposed to be paying for all of this?"

"Well, normally you would. But considering that putting you on my Federally registered books would be about the dumbest move we could make right now, I'm working pro bono for the time being. Maybe when this whole thing blows over, we can negotiate some kind of compensation."

"You're seriously expecting me to compensate you for this fiasco?"

"Maybe we could consider it as an incentive for me *not* to just dump you on some backwater rock that hasn't developed sentient lifeforms yet."

"Is that a threat?"

"Oh, jeez. Look, Alexander, I admit that I'm in the wrong as much as you are, but I'm no underhanded schnook. If I was, I'd have just hit the passenger eject button-"

Here he haphazardly gestured a little too close to said button.

"-as soon as it was obvious that you were going to be a problem, but I didn't. I'm a professional with a reputation to uphold, and more than that, I'm a sentient Yoplengir capable of basic compassion. I'm not going to try and take advantage of you. But at the same time, I'm taking a loss for now, and I can only cover so many expenses."

"I guess I can appreciate that," Alexander grumbled. "Though, at the risk of worsening my own predicament further, I don't have any cash with me, I'm now apparently out of a job, and even if I got my one bag of belongings back, I have no idea what's valuable in the Federation. Unless there's some way you can charge my credit card or access my bank account back on Earth, I'm basically broke."

"Yeah, that is a bit of a problem. In theory, every planet's individual currencies have a set conversion rate to the Federal Groat, but you can just imagine how long it takes to work out a new addition to that scheme. It'll probably be a few yelaageroos before we figure out what your Earth money is even worth. Never fear, though. We can probably come up with some kind of arrangement before then."

Ryan scratched the side of his head. Suddenly his eye lit up as if he had been struck by the good idea fairy.

"You know... there *are* other forms of compensation that aren't simply monetary. From what I gather, you *do* have a particular set of skills."

Alexander shot him a look.

"Are you seriously suggesting what I think you're suggesting?"

"Hey well, I mean. You apparently managed to not only impress a Grand Master with your uh, '*prowess*', but you briefly got yourself hired by the Chancellor based on your '*performance.*' If you ask me, you certainly appear to be capable of '*generating a valuable commodity.*'"

"Ryan, I don't mean to tell you how to drive, but I'd feel a hell of a lot better if you didn't take your hands off the wheel to do those air quotes like that."

"Oh, sorry," he said, putting his hands back on the wheel. "Point is, Alexander, lacking any '*goods*', perhaps we can negotiate more along the '*services*' line."

Alexander screwed his eyes shut and sighed as Ryan waggled his eyebrow.

"Okay Ryan. Listen, there's something I have to tell you."

"If you don't want to, that's alright!" Ryan interrupted. "I am perfectly happy with working out something else that doesn't involve any funny business. But hey, you know, it's not every day I get a shot at someone who's even come within spitting distance of a Grand Master, much less dotted his i's and crossed his t's, if you know what I mean. All *I'd* ever ask for is a quick hand job and call it square. Heck, I'd even throw in a free breakfast at IGOW!"

"What's IGOW?"

"The Intergalactic Grotto of Waffles! Best dang waffles you'll ever eat in your entire life!"

Alexander sat still for a moment. His stomach grumbled, and he realized it had been quite some time since breakfast. From the way things were looking, who knows how he'd be able to sort out getting meals from this point on. Plus, he always loved a good waffle.

'God, I'm honestly considering this.' He thought to himself.

"Ugh... *Just* a hand job?" he asked reluctantly. "I can't believe I'm asking this, but what exactly kind of agreement are you proposing?"

"Well, I'd give you a standard kidnapping package. That includes cost of transportation, a two-week stay at a motel that probably won't sell your organs, a couple of meal tickets, and I'm throwing in an extra IGOW breakfast for free. That'll square us up on what you technically owe, and I also won't press charges over false engagement of a service for hire."

"Hardy-har-har. How much is all that?"

"Not counting the breakfast, I usually charge 2 and 752,981 over 2,000,000 Groats for the lot."

"Come again?"

"That's 2 Groats, 1 Farthing, 3 Testoons, 6 Quids, 17 Bob. I've got a handy chart here if you want to double-check the math on that."

Ryan reached back behind his seat and dug around for a bit, eventually pulling out a picture frame housing a somewhat wonky embroidered table of coinage values.

1 Groat	13 Farthings	21 Testoons	364 Quids	21,476 Bob
1/13 Groat	1 Farthing	1 & 1,231/2,000 Testoons	28 Quids	1,652 Bob
1/21 Groat	6189/10,000 Farthing	1 Testoon	17 & 823/2,500 Quids	1,022 & 1,057/2,500 Bob
13/5,000 Groat	1/28 Farthing	577/10,000 Testoon	1 Quid	59 Bob
93/2,000,000 Groat	1/1,652 Farthing	9/10,000 Testoon	1/59 Quid	1 Bob
All conversions rounded to the ten-thousandth, except for Bob.				

Alexander stared at it for a moment but almost immediately felt a headache coming on. Math had never exactly been his strong suit, and even if it had, the fractions on display would still have been horrendous.

"Right..." he said. "Well, I *guess* that doesn't sound like the worst deal on planet Earth. Or... space. But wouldn't that be considered prostitution? Is that even legal in the Federation?"

"If we were exchanging actual Federal currency, then yes. However, all properly licensed, bonded, and insured prostitutes are supposed to be commissioned under the Federal Office for the Procurement of Propositional Employment and Regulation of Yodelers, which is more hoops than we'd want to jump through, considering we're sort of on the lamb at the moment. Seeing as how we're simply trading one favor for another, I think we can get away with an 'Exchange of Services Among Friends or Business Associates' contract."

"God, what is with this obsession with paperwork in the Federation?" Alexander exclaimed.

"Personally," Ryan whispered conspiratorially. "Aside from getting to put their fancy, decorative pens to good use, I think the bureaucrats are slowly attempting to regulate everything to paper, up to the point where the physical multiverse itself is rendered down to words on a page. Much easier to legislate, I imagine."

Smig couldn't tell if he was pulling his leg or trying to be serious.

"Well, that aside. Wouldn't the Chancellor be able to track us down if we start filing contracts? How is that any better than your pay books?"

"It's way easier to obfuscate the details with favor contracts. Monetary transactions and records have very strict requirements for the details you need to provide and need to be reported promptly. Favor contracts have enough leeway to leave certain facts just vague enough that they'd have a tricky time tracing it back to its origin, even if they noticed it in the first place."

"Do we even have to bother submitting a contract into the system at all?"

"Oh, yeah!" Ryan said with conviction. "Snubbing the Chancellor is asking for some real trouble, but it's not *technically* illegal. Intentionally attempting to circumvent the bureaucracy is *absolutely* illegal, and it's prosecuted with extreme prejudice. Trust me, dumping a few breadcrumbs in the system is risky, but it's a far cry better than having a starving antpanther drag us screaming down into its lair, wanting to know where our form D59-23's are. Any other questions?"

"I guess not," Alexander replied. "It's just... I don't know. I'm starving, and I don't like running up debts, but giving a practical stranger a hand job is kind of on the edge of my comfort level."

"Hey, again, no pressure or compulsion on my part. We can work something out eventually."

They flew on in silence for a while. Alexander sat brewing things over in his mind.

"Oh, fuck it," he said. "I've done worse things than give someone a hand job, though I'm usually not sober for it."

"You'll do it?"

"Sure, what the hell. I'm getting more out of it than the one time Jake Travis had me '*borrow*' a hole saw from work to drill a hole in one of the stalls at the Leaky Goose."

"Awesome! Sign here."

At the press of a button, a screen and stylus popped out in front of Alexander.

"Did you already have this contract written up?" he asked suspiciously.

"It was auto-generated from the computer listening to our conversation."

"The computers are listening to us? Are you *really* sure the Chancellor isn't tracking us down even as we speak?"

"Could the Chancellor of Earth pull up the records at your local DMV if he wanted to track you down and slug you for insulting his mother?"

"They have DMVs in the Federation?" Smig asked incredulously.

"Oh, come on! I don't know what kind of planet you're from, but is it such a surprise that Digital Monkey Vendors are universal? I can't imagine a space-faring society capable of functioning without them!"

"Uh..."

"In any case," Ryan continued. "We haven't done anything illegal, so *any* kind of record keeper wouldn't be obligated to give personal information out to politicians just willy-nilly! So as long as we keep *mostly* within the boundaries of the law, we're dealing with statistical odds that are astronomically weighted in our favor."

"Yeah, like that meteoroid we hit earlier," Alexander muttered under his breath.

Alexander glanced over the contract. It was suitably dense in its legalese to be beyond his complete grasp, but it did not appear to have anything that would royally screw him over at the first opportunity. He took the stylus and put his name on the line underneath Ryan's clearly unpracticed signature.

"There," Alexander said. "So... you want to take care of that when we land, or..?"

"That's an option. I can also set us on autopilot for a while if you'd rather not build up a sense of impending doom over the inevitable."

"While you're flying?"

"Look, its deep space. There's barely any obstacles to begin with, and now that I've remembered to turn on the proximity alert system, we'll get alarm bells ringing before anything sizable comes within 26 light-yelaageroos of us."

Alexander sighed.

"Yeah, alright. Let's just get this over with."

"Sweet, gimme a second."

"Don't make this any weirder than it has to be, okay?"

"Don't worry, I just have to get situated."

Ryan pressed a few buttons and thumped another console, which seemed to set the autopilot. Shuffling around in his seat, Ryan then tugged at his waistline, suddenly revealing the line of a pair of pants that had blended in so seamlessly that Alexander had thought the alien was unabashedly nude. Honestly, even with the pants drawn down, the only appreciable difference before and after was the strange, globular ▮▮▮▮ *{ZUCCHINI}* that was now exposed. Alexander tried not to stare, but there was no escaping the awkwardness of the situation.

"Okay, ready to go!" Ryan proclaimed.

Alexander frowned but decided to keep any dumb questions to himself for now. He'd probably only get dumb answers in reply anyway. Reaching over, he gave Ryan's ▮▮▮▮ *{ZUCCHINI}* an exploratory poke. It was warm and rubbery.

'God. What am I getting myself into.' Alexander thought to himself.

Wrapping his fingers around the alien's ▮▮▮▮ *{ZUCCHINI}*, he tested the waters with a few strokes.

"Mmm," Ryan murmured. "That's good, but uh... pick up the pace a little. I like things rough."

A little embarrassed, Alexander turned away to stare at the console in front of him as he ██████ {*PERFORMED MANUAL OSCILLATION OF THE DIGITS*} a little more vigorously.

"Yeah... Yeah, harder." Ryan said.

Alexander couldn't help pulling a bit of a face as he complied, pulling a little quicker and a little more forcefully. Ryan's █████ {*ZUCCHINI*} seemed to stretch in his hands like a weird rubber ██████ {*ZUCCHINI*}.

"Ahh, yeah," Ryan said through heavy breaths. "Come on. Harder than that. Yank on it good."

Alexander gave him a dubious sideways glance. He thought he was going at it pretty hard now, but he upped the ante anyway. Ryan squirmed in his seat.

"Good. Getting closer. Really pull on it."

"I don't want to hurt anything," Alexander said, deliberately trying to look at anything but what his hand was doing.

"It's fine! I can take it! Gimme some good yanks!"

Alexander now had his full arm active in the motion, his hand slapping loudly at Ryan's base.

"Come on!" Ryan practically shouted. "I'm almost there! Give it one big, *super yank!*"

Not without a little frustration, Alexander gave a final wrench. Ryan's █████ {*ZUCCHINI*} nearly stretched far enough to bump into the dashboard. Suddenly there was a loud 'POP!' like a champagne cork. Alexander's hand slammed into the steering wheel, and he only briefly stared in surprise at the floppy, green, disembodied ████ {*ZUCCHINI*} in his hand before Ryan let loose with a whooping scream.

"WHAAAAOOOO!"

Alexander joined in on the screaming as he shot back in his seat and wildly flung the dismembered ████ {*ZUCCHINI*} in panic. It bounced like an oversized, undercooked asparagus around the cockpit as the two occupants flailed around like chickens with freshly misplaced heads.

"AAAaaa- Got ya!" Ryan suddenly shouted.

This sudden halt got Alexander to stop screaming just long enough to open one eye and look over at Ryan, who was now remarkably calm given the circumstances.

"Ho ho! I got you good!" Ryan exclaimed, now starting to giggle.

"What?" Alexander asked in shock.

"I got you with the old fake ████ {ZUCCHINI} gag! You were tugging on a dildo the entire time! My real ████ {ZUCCHINI} was over here!"

"Are you shitting me?"

"No, see?"

"God! No! Put that fucking thing away!"

Ryan laughed in earnest now, rolling in his seat in a fit. Alexander stared unbelievingly around the ship. The expired dildo had unfortunately come to rest on the dashboard directly in front of him, so he turned to look out the passenger window.

"Oh, golly!" Ryan said, almost crying between fits. "The look on your face when it popped out! Oh, lordy! Hee hee, ha!"

Alexander rubbed his face with open palms as Ryan's merriment continued unabated. He'd fallen for some monumentally dumb pranks in his time, but this one just took the cake.

"Real funny," Alexander said with heavy sarcasm.

"You bet your garbanzos! That was hilarious!" Ryan said, gasping for breath. "But seriously, It's been a while since someone fell for that so *perfectly*. Oh, that was great."

"Yeah, well, you can rip up that contract, bub. I'm not doing you any more favors."

"That's the beauty of it!" Ryan giggled again. "If you'd have dug deep enough between the lines, you could have figured out that you were actually obligated to be the recipient of a prank the entire time! No actual hand jobs required!"

"Are you serious? You wrote a deceptive contract for a *prank*?"

"Oh, lighten up. Everybody does that. That's why it's generally polite not to read too deeply into the fine print on small contracts between friends. Don't want to be a spoilsport, after all."

"I can't fucking believe this."

"I don't know if the guys at the IGOW will believe it either, but I'm sure as shooting going to tell them all about it!"

Alexander fully buried his face in his hands and groaned.

"For real?" he asked through his fingers.

"Yup! I included a clause for bragging rights in schedule A9-24.6."

Smig sighed, but as mad and embarrassed as he was, he secretly had to admit it was one hell of a prank to pull off.

"Of course you did," he replied.

"Cheer up, Alexander! You worked your way out of a debt without actually performing any sexual favors. Man, even without the contractual obligations, I'd buy you breakfast anyways. That was fantastic!"

"How much longer until we're there?" Alexander asked.

"Not long!" Ryan replied. "It should be within sight here soon!"

"Not soon enough."

{EDITORIAL NOTE: Given Lord Mipper-Hum-Bailicorn's irrational insistence that 'all nouns be zucchini' and his refusal to back down, the right honorable member has been sacked. We deeply apologize again for this gross misconduct and trust it shall not happen again under the personal supervision of Klerman Dwahoogaloo, Chief of B.A.S.T.A.R.D.S.}

Chapter 8
The Breakfast

It wasn't long before a strange asteroid came into view. The rocky surface couldn't have been more than half a mile in diameter, but its reach was bolstered by the long, skinny landing docks sticking out in numerous directions. The whole impression was something like a yacht marina designed by M.C. Escher. All of these converged on a structure that looked like a shopping mall had been folded over on top of itself and squished down to sit as compact as possible. Bright signage flashed strange pictures and symbols into the void. More than a few of these flickered in ways that seemed to suggest poor maintenance.

"So, what all is on that little rock?" Alexander asked, trying to move swiftly on from events recently transpired.

"Pretty much anything you might need," Ryan replied. "There's a gas station, a diner, a motel, a hardware store, a post office, a library, a public notary, a private notary, a private eye, a public eye, a pub, a prive. Too much to list."

"Is it going to have, like, a breathable atmosphere and gravity and all that?"

"Oh yeah, of course!"

"That's good. Come to think of it, is it just coincidence that everyone in the Federation seems to have the same basic needs as Earthlings?"

"Well... yes and no. There's plenty of lifeforms in the Federation that have more extreme survival requirements, such as the Belkerns, who need to be constantly submerged in chlorine trifluoride in order to live. In general, however, *most* life is similar enough that you can have just a handful of standard atmospheres. There's no *intentional* segregation built into the system, outside of the assumption that most folks don't want to be put into an environment where they'll explode."

"Explode?"

"Oh, jeez yeah. Those Belkerns would go right up if they ever visited a sandy beach or an asbestos factory. But don't worry about it! I've been to this station before and seeing as you haven't passed out in the scooter yet, you should be fine down there. Hang on a sec while I grab the parking slip."

They pulled up to a little booth floating in orbit around the station. An accordion tube extended out towards the scooter and magnetically suction-cupped itself to Ryan's door. After a few minutes of digging around to find the screwdriver, Ryan cranked the window down and plucked a little paper ticket from the booth. This done, and the window laboriously wound back up, they came in to dock among a strange hodge-podge of similarly sized ships.

"All right, you are now free to remove your- oh, you didn't have the extra restraint belts buckled."

"Extra restraint belts?" Alexander asked.

"Yeah, you got the one that goes across your shoulder and waist, but there's like, three more to do up. That must've made bumping into that random meteoroid a *lot* less comfortable."

"Now you tell me. I'm used to just one seat belt in most vehicles."

"Don't take this the wrong way, Alexander, but I feel that either *you* need to start making fewer assumptions, or *I* need to start pointing out more things that seem obvious to me."

"I'd rather just ask dumb questions if it's all the same to you," Alexander replied dryly.

"Fine with me."

"How do I get out of here?"

"Just to leave the scooter normally or in an emergency?"

"Just to leave the scooter normally."

"Okay. *Not* the handle that you grabbed onto when we took off. That's *supposed* to eject your seat in case of emergency, but it's been kind of sticky recently. The small handle down by your arm is for the door."

Alexander scrambled out of the scooter, vowing never to set foot in it again if he could help it. Ryan followed him out, taking only a brief moment to set a padlock onto a barn latch screwed into the driver's door. With a click and a tug to make sure it was secure, he leapt up to the walking platform next to Alexander.

"Nice security system," Alexander remarked.

"Oh, that? No, the padlock is just to keep the door from swinging open. The back window will fall out if you so much as cough too close to it, so I don't worry about locking it up anymore."

With that, Ryan started wandering off towards the central hub. Smig stared at the death trap in which he had traveled through the inky void of space.

"You coming, Alexander?" he called out.

Alexander walked quickly to catch up to the little green blob. The long dock reminded him of a passenger walkway between airport terminals, only there weren't any of those convenient moving sidewalks. The two of them wandered through an assortment of aliens milling back and forth down the long corridor. There were quite a number of oddities present, sporting all manner of strange limbs and bodily features, but Alexander couldn't help but notice *again* that none of them were nearly as unusual as the Envoy, Yerligam Snauper of Glunt, had been.

None of these passersby seemed to take much notice of either him or Ryan and eventually, they emerged into an area that felt like a cramped strip mall court. The space was diamond shaped and rose past two floors to a glass ceiling where you could almost make out some stars beyond the glare of the advertisements. Every possible inch of wall space was taken up by storefronts of some kind or another, and the whole place was buzzing with activity.

Having worked in construction, Alexander's attention was drawn to some of the more unusual architectural features of the building, such as the levitating fountain in the center of the diamond and the light fixtures that seemed to be made of some kind of glowing fluid. He wondered why, in the name of all that was holy, popcorn ceilings could still be a thing even out in space until he noticed that the little clumps were slowly milling around like bees in a hive. Staring at them gave Alexander the heebie-jeebies, especially when they started staring back, so he quickly followed Ryan as he moved on to other parts of the building.

"Wait... Are those full spiral escalators?" Alexander asked.

"Yup! Saves a lot of space. Just don't trip on 'em, whatever you do. The IGOW's just beyond them over there."

"Wow. You know, I was thinking it sounded a bit like a diner chain we have on Earth, but I swear that almost looks like an exact copy. Do they do pancakes?"

"What's a pancake?"

"Uh, you know. Like a flapjack?"

"Never heard of them."

"Really? Well, I think you use basically the same batter as waffles, but you cook them on a regular frying pan instead of the waffle iron."

"Just on a pan? Wouldn't they be, like, flat and floppy?"

"Yeah, exactly."

"Huh. I don't know. If it doesn't have the little holes for holding the pâté, that just sounds like it would be disappointing."

Ryan was already in the door before Alexander could balk at the idea of pâté on a waffle. A waitress with five or six reticulated tentacles and a seemingly permanent look of abject apathy on her face waved them over to a pair of stools at the counter. Alexander sat down next to Ryan and stared around the establishment. The entire restaurant was full of foreign sights and smells, but at the very least, the waffles looked like normal waffles.

"You want me to order for you?" Ryan asked. "I know a couple items on their secret menu."

"Uh, No thanks. I'd rather work it out myself."

Alexander stared at the laminated menu for a bit.

"Though, I might need you to help translate. I can't read any of this."

"Oh! Here, hang on."

Ryan flicked the menu with his fingers a few times. All of the words jumbled around and reluctantly fizzled into English before his eyes.

"That better?"

"Whoa, yeah."

"Sometimes, these cheap printouts take a little persuasion to work right."

"Hey, Ryan," the waitress cut in without any trace of even mock enthusiasm. "You want your usual?"

"You betcha Wyrmbs! That and whatever he's having."

"Uh..." Alexander stammered, caught off guard.

His eyes darted all over the menu while Wyrmbs gave him the sort of look a dead fish would be envious of.

"I'll do... a number 42."

"We're all out of 42," Wyrmbs replied. "Apologies for the inconvenience."

"Okay, uh... a number 36?"

"You want bean butter or beef spread with that?" Wyrmbs asked.

"Uh, none if that's all right."

"Either of you want drinks?"

"Cough-E® for me," Ryan answered.

"I'll stick with water," Alexander said, figuring that was the least potentially hazardous option.

Wyrmbs made some kind of noise and wandered off.

"Glad we caught Wyrmbs," Ryan said. "You know how sometimes you'll go to a diner, and the service wants to take your order before you've even had a chance to look at your menu, only to disappear off the face of the asteroid for twenty yelaageroos? Then when they finally *do* show up, the food's cold, and half of it wasn't even what you ordered! Not here, though. Good old Wyrmbs takes care of her customers."

Alexander frowned again. He'd just thought of something.

"How did she know your name was Ryan?" he asked.

"I come here a lot."

"But you changed your name on the way here."

"Yeah, but she never forgets a face."

"That doesn't explai-"

"Order up!" Wyrmbs called out.

In a flash, Wyrmbs served up each of their plates, refilled Ryan's mug, topped off Alexander's ice water, set down an elaborate wire rack with about eighteen different unidentifiable goops and pastes and slapped the bill on the counter between them.

"Thanks, Wyrmbs!" Ryan called after her. "Well, Alexander. Dig in!"

Ryan had already taken a thick scoop of something brown with tan flecks from the rack and was smearing it across his waffles. Alexander looked over the assortment of toppings and decided not to risk it. Taking a test bite, he had to admit that it was indeed one of the best waffles he'd ever had, even plain. Hungry as he was, it didn't take long for him to finish off his plate.

"Good, huh?" Ryan asked between mouthfuls.

"Yeah, you were right. Those are damn good waffles. So, we're hanging around here for a while?"

"Yup. We can go wander around the promenade after this if you want. There's a shop off in the back corner I'd like to-"

Ryan was suddenly cut off by someone dropping a heavy pair of hands on his and Alexander's shoulders. Before either of them had a chance to react, they both were forcibly swung around to come face to face with a large fellow who could best be described as a cross between a gorilla, a bullfrog, and an atretochoana eiselti. Behind him was a skinny alien who just looked like something halfway between a salamander and a shaved chipmunk.

"Well, well. If it isn't Ryan Schmidtke," the salamander-chipmunk hybrid said in a voice that sounded like it came more from his nasal cavity than his mouth.

"Blusoh!" Ryan laughed nervously. "I -ngh, see Gerald's grip is as strong as ever. What are you guys doing here?"

"Oh, you know," Blusoh replied. "We were just out running a few errands for the boss when we happened to see our old pal having breakfast at the IGOW. You know we just had to swing by for a little chat."

"Oh, gee. You guys didn't have to take a break from work just to say hi to little old me. Heh, heh. Are you, uh, still working for old Kalipper?"

"Nope. He retired after that last kerfuffle you were involved in. We're working for Baron Zloykot now."

"Oh beans," Ryan looked especially nervous now. "Out of all the people I could have hoped you were working for, he has got to be on the bottom of my list."

"That's funny because Zloykot has you right at the top of *his* list." Blusoh chuckled menacingly.

Gerald, the big bullfrog that was holding them, gave an out-of-place, high-pitched, tittering giggle. Blusoh stopped laughing and stared at him.

"Gad, Gerald. Your laugh always gives me the creeps," Blusoh said.

Gerald simply blinked.

"Hey, listen, guys," Ryan squeaked. "I know that Zloykot and I have some problems that need to be sorted out eventually, but you couldn't have caught me at a worse time. You would not believe the predicament I've gotten myself in."

"You're right! I wouldn't," Blusoh replied bluntly. "Gerald, take Ryan out to the scooter while I take care of their bill."

Alexander had been trying to decide whether or not to open his mouth, but now that Gerald effortlessly plucked both him and Ryan up, one in each hand, tucked them under his arms, and started lumbering for the door, he wasn't in a position to do much of anything. Gerald's fur wasn't particularly unpleasant outside of being smooshed right into his face, and Smig struggled only enough to keep it out of his mouth. Carried at an odd angle, legs dangling, they were bobbed and jostled around before Gerald unceremoniously dumped them into the padded trunk of a small ship. The enormous gorilla slapped the lid shut, leaving them in pitch darkness.

Chapter 9
The Kidnapping

"What in the ever-loving hell just happened?" Alexander asked, trying to get his bearings in the dark trunk.

"We've just been kidnapped," Ryan replied. "And I'll bet you anything that Blusoh's not going to get my parking validated."

"Seriously, *what* is going on? Who are those guys? How do *they* know your new name?"

"Calm down! Blusoh and Gerald are a couple of cronies for hire. They've got nothing against me personally. They just have a bad habit of working for people who do."

"That's fantastic!" Alexander growled. "How much trouble have you gotten me into now?"

"*Well...* If they had still been working for old Kalipper, not so bad. I just forgot to pick up his dry cleaning before the late fees kicked in. Now Zloykot, that's a different matter entirely. He's a drug baron with connections to the space mafia."

"Oh, that sounds great!" Alexander said with sarcastic enthusiasm. "What'd you do to piss him off?"

"Nothing intentional! There was this whole misunderstanding where I kidnapped his daughter-"

"Are you serious?"

"*Professionally*, for cripes' sake! Listen, she did the whole bit by the book on my end, so I thought it was just a regular job at first. The thing I didn't know was that she'd told Zloykot that she was eloping with some nut job just to piss him off. Of course, by the time we got to the motel, she had changed her mind and wanted to go back home. She called him from my own scooter phone to ask if he could pick her up. Now he not only thinks I tried to steal his daughter, he thinks I botched the job! Me! A professional kidnapper screwing up something like that!"

Alexander was still trying to find some way of adequately expressing his complete and utter bewilderment when the vehicle suddenly twisted around and sent the two of them rolling around. Both he and Ryan squirmed blindly in the dark.

"For the love of all that's holy, please tell me we're not going to wind up dead," Alexander grunted.

"Okay. We're not going to wind up dead," Ryan squeaked from the corner of the trunk he had been shoved into.

"Somehow, that didn't make me feel any better."

"Don't worry, Alexander. I've gotten myself out of a few sticky situations before."

"My confidence is at an all-time hi- what the hell is that!?"

"What is what?" Ryan asked.

"Something weird and rubbery just bounced off of my hand!"

"Whoops! I think my other decoy slipped out."

"Other decoy? Do you have *another* dildo? Where the hell do you even keep- actually, don't tell me because I don't want to know!"

After what seemed like an excessive amount of bumping around in the dark, the scooter finally smoothed out and came to a stop.

"Alright, Schmidtke," Blusoh's muffled voice called from outside. "We're gonna open the trunk and take you to the boss. No funny business. Gerald's got his womping gloves on."

"Seriously!" Alexander whispered. "How does everyone know your name if you just changed it."

"Is *that* what you're going to focus on?" Ryan replied indignantly. "You do *not* handle crisis situations very well."

Sudden light blinded them as the trunk opened to reveal Gerald's fine pleather gloves reaching in to pluck them out. Once again, they were roughly tucked up under the burly alien's arms and manhandled away. Alexander couldn't see much except for a remarkably hairy armpit and occasional glimpses of the carpet, which honestly didn't look much different. Before long, they were unceremoniously dumped out on the floor. Gathering their wits, they found themselves in a large, fancy hall filled with extravagant decorations and trappings of wealth. At the far end of the room was a raised platform that supported an exceptionally luxurious chaise lounge.

Reclined on top of this was a menacing, muscular creature who looked something like a striped tiger, but instead of fur, it seemed to have gleaming skin like honey-colored gelatin. He lay relaxed with one arm propping himself up, the other crisscrossed, holding the end of a strange, hookah-like device. Leisurely drawing from the tip, he let loose a long draft of smoke from his nostrils, which poured down the dais and rolled out across the floor like a heavy fog. Hardly moving, save for the occasional rolling flick of his tail, he looked Ryan and Alexander over with deep, glowing red eyes.

Blusoh cautiously approached.

"Baron Zloykot, please forgive the interruption. As you can see, we ran into a friend of yours while we- what the hell? Who are *you*?"

Blusoh had turned to gesture at Ryan but was now staring straight at Alexander.

"Uh, me?" Alexander asked, not liking the sudden attention at all.

"Yes, you! Were you in the room before?"

"No... I was with Ryan at the diner."

"Oh, for fuck's sake. Did Gerald pick you up too? Jeez, I gotta start doing laps around the guy before we take off. He's so big that, half the time, I don't notice that he's holding onto someone."

"He's with me, Blusoh," Ryan piped up.

Blusoh glanced back and forth between the two. Alexander decided to shrug and shake his head to Ryan's apparent consternation. The Weasel sighed and leaned in close to Smig.

"I'm sorry about all this," he whispered. "Just sit tight for a bit, and we'll get you taken care of."

Blusoh turned back to the baron.

"Apologies for the kerfuffle, sir. Would you care to have a word with Mr. Schmidtke?"

Zloykot simply lowered his head, staring intently at Ryan. Blusoh turned and gestured to Gerald, who began herding both of his charges right up to the imposing figure.

"Gerald! No! Not that one! We only need- ugh..." Blusoh cut himself off with a sigh and gave up.

Ryan and Alexander found themselves face to face with the baron. His eyes didn't quite seem to give off heat like the Chancellor's had, but they certainly were a bright, glaring red.

"Ah, hah hah. Hello, Zloykot!" Ryan said timidly. "Listen, I know that every time someone tells you that there's been a misunderstanding, you've flown into a horrific rage, and the offenders are never seen again in one piece, so I'm *not* going to tell you that there's been a misunderstanding. *However*, I think this is an excellent opportunity for us to run through all of the facts one more time and make sure we have everything straightened out."

"Straightened out?" Zloykot asked, drawing the question out with a deep, growling rumble.

"Yeah, straightened out! Again, no misunderstandings. But it's come to my attention that some of the facts may have been um... poorly represented."

The baron let loose a deep-breasted chuckle. This carried on into a menacing laugh. Which then carried on a little bit longer than it should have. Then abruptly, he stopped and glared at both of them before breaking down alltogether into a loud, snorting giggle that he seemed unable to stop. Zloykot's hookah mouthpiece clattered to the ground as he ran his hands over his face in a futile attempt to pull himself together, which only served to weirdly distort his head in an unnervingly squishy way. Alexander and Ryan exchanged glances as the alien continued his uncontrollable mirth.

"Hang on, he's higher than a Kalepsian kite!" Ryan exclaimed.

"On his own supply, too," Blusoh muttered through a facepalm. "This is just fantastic. I should've come in and checked on him beforehand."

"What's he trading these days anyway?" Ryan asked, shuffling a little.

"Some kind of weird hybrid I don't remember the name of. I think it's basically saffron smoke drawn through absinthe or something like that."

"That sounds more likely to make you sick than get you high," Alexander grimaced.

"Maybe for you," Blusoh said. "But not for Zloykot. I don't think there's a drug in the known multiverse that could give him so much as a hangover. Slygers just don't suffer detrimental effects like most folks do."

"Aside from the 'getting high' part," Ryan remarked.

"Well yeah," Blusoh admitted.

While they were talking, Ryan had taken the opportunity to wiggle his way out of Gerald's grasp and up to the drug baron.

"Hey, Zloykot!" he called out. "How ya doing, pal?"

The baron's giggling subsided a little but didn't absolutely cease as his reddened eyes lazily drifted to focus on the green blob in front of him.

"How am I- heh heh heh, doing?" the drug lord asked, definitely out of the loop.

"Yeah, pal," Ryan addressed him in a 'buddy-like' tone. "Seems like you're doing pretty well for yourself."

Ryan cautiously rested an elbow up against the chaise lounge.

"Genuine faux-squirrel-tail furniture," he observed admiringly. "Hagal quartz plinths, upsidaisium chandelier, naturally shed alicorn toothpicks. Must have been working pretty hard for you to get yourself up to this point."

"Ryan," Alexander whispered. "What the hell are you doing?"

"Why just catching up with my old pal Zloykot of course!" he replied in about the most unconvincing manner possible. "This silly old slyger and me go way back, after all! *Clearly*, he's just pulling a prank, and the two of you don't need to worry about keeping me and Alexander here tied up any-"

Without warning, and to the surprise of everyone, Zloykot ate Ryan. Literally just opened his mouth and slurped him up. Ryan had no time to react as the gelatin-like structure of the slyger stretched around his ovaloid body and swallowed him whole.

"*Judas fucking priest!*" Alexander shouted, scrambling to hide behind Gerald.

"Oh for Glob's sake. This is snowballing into the greatest shit show of all time," Blusoh said through another facepalm, this time with both hands.

"He just fucking *ate* him!" Alexander exclaimed.

"Yeah, well, I guess Zloykot had the munchies. Glob damn it. I told him to go easy with his medication."

"Medication!?"

"Yeah, that saffron stuff isn't supposed to be recreational. That is unless *someone* around here decides to quadruple their dose for the afternoon!"

Zloykot cackled at the weasel's disapproving face for a bit before flopping himself over and giggling up at the ceiling.

"What the hell do we do?" Alexander asked.

"Turn off his hookah and get him to come back down eventually," Blusoh replied.

"I mean about Ryan. He's been *eaten!*"

"Calm down, buckaroo. Slygers don't have a digestive system. I dunno why they get hungry, but everything they eat just comes right back out in a couple hours."

Alexander peered around Gerald and tried to formulate some semblance of rationality.

"Well... won't he suffocate?"

"Nah, slygers are porous," Blusoh said. "Seriously, we're all safer if we just let nature take its course and don't try to take his food away from him. Ryan will come out just fine. Of course, by that time, Zloykot might be in a better frame of mind to be pissed off at him again, but that's something else. The question now is, what are we going to do with *you*? You got any reason to be valuable to us?"

"What?"

"Look, I know that *we're* the ones who screwed up, but speaking as unionized members of Cronies for Hire, we've got a reputation to uphold. We've got connections to the Space Mafia after all, and if folks got it into their head that we'd let any accidental captives just slip away, we'd be ruined! You got any rich relatives? Hell, any poor relatives we could give a temporary loan to so it looks like they're rich?"

"Uh... no. Not to speak of."

Blusoh scratched his head.

"How about a job?" he asked. "Maybe you work for somebody with Mafia insurance?"

"No... Well, I guess *technically* I do work for somebody, but that's probably not-"

"Who?"

"You know, I don't think it'd be a good idea to get them involved. It's kind of a complicated situation."

"Look, Joe Shmoe, I'm doing you a favor by trying to negotiate here. We could just as easily *enhance* our reputation by making sure you stay disappeared for a lot longer."

Smig glanced up at Gerald's unblinking eyes. They seemed less like the stone-cold eyes of a killer than the blank, off-kilter stare of Homer Simpson, but still, he had no doubt that these two were capable of some pretty shady deals.

"All right," Alexander said with resignation. "Here, check out my ID card."

Alexander held out the card to Blusoh. The alien squinted over the writing only for a moment before his eyes suddenly bugged out of his head.

"Holy fuck!" he shouted hysterically. "You're the *Chancellor's concubine*!?"

"Uh, yeah," Alexander said. "That's the one."

"Crap baskets! We just kidnapped a concubine from Chancellor Bulbeeyoog!"

"Yup."

"H-Hey listen, I thought you were just some ordinary chump! If we had known you were in the Chancellor's retinue, I'd have at least, uh... made Gerald comb his hair or something."

"Oh, that's uh... no problem."

"Look, *now* we've got an even bigger problem. If the Chancellor finds out about this, we're liable to figure out just how quickly the supreme leader of the universe can shove an order for an 'armed intervention with extreme prejudice' down the bureaucracy's throat! For the love of Globbo, please tell me you'll work with us on this! I'm not ending up like my Uncle Shmukle."

"Uh, what happened to Uncle Shmukle?"

"He once had the opportunity to answer a question asked by the Chancellor himself." Blusoh said in a grave tone. "No one knows exactly what he said. All the official commission could tell us after the fact was that..."

The weasel stood stock still, staring off into the distance.

"He fibbed."

Alexander blinked.

"And?" he asked.

"And the Chancellor found out." Blusoh stated.

Gerald shivered. Smig looked around and noticed that even Baron Zloykot had fallen silent.

"So!" Blusoh exclaimed. "We gotta work out some way of passing this off as a PR stunt or something that's all above board."

"A PR stunt?" Alexander asked incredulously.

"Yeah, you know. Like we hired you to make it *look* like we kidnapped you, to pick up some major street cred."

"So... you just do up a contract and slip me some cash or something?"

"Sure, but we've got to throw in something pretty flashy too. Kidnappings happen every day, after all, and we need something that'll convince people that we're milking this for all it's got. Let me think here..."

Blusoh suddenly arched his eyebrows in a way that suggested he had just been visited by the good idea fairy. All that was missing was the light bulb above his head.

"Say..." he said, thoughtfully rubbing his chin. "You've got a, uh... '*particular skill set*,' don't you? Maybe we can utilize that with the boss while he's mostly comatose."

"*Really?*" Alexander asked incredulously. "Is this a thing with being a concubine? Everybody asks for sexual favors? And with whatever the hell that guy is?"

"Listen," Blusoh replied, cradling his hands together. "I understand that you're a professional and that this sort of thing should not be an expectation. However, I'm also trying to be nice and come up with something we can all work with, and I know next to nothing about you. Maybe you have some other talents or attributes we can work with, like, I don't know, underwater basket weaving. It'd be kinda weird to kidnap a concubine and just have you weave a wet basket for us, but hey. Maybe the basket is nicely detailed, and people will be impressed by the plaiting. If you don't want to do any dirty deeds, that's A-okay, but do you have anything else we can consider?"

Alexander exhaled through his nostrils. Surely he could come up with something better than screwing around with a stoned-out gelatin cat.

"I don't know! About the only other thing I have any *real* experience in is construction. I don't suppose you guys need a wall knocked out, or a deck built, or something?"

"Eh, Zloykot just finished a load of renovations. I don't think there's a whole lot to work with there."

"Well, uh... I guess I can do some nifty tricks with a tape measure."

"Using the word '*nifty*' to describe something does not exactly scream '*street cred worthy*.'"

"*You're* the one who suggested underwater basket weaving." Smig retorted indignantly.

"At least that'd give us something we can display. Imagine trying to impress someone by telling them about some '*nifty*' tape measure tricks that you saw once."

"Fair, I suppose," Alexander conceded. "But you wouldn't be able to display me jacking someone off, either."

A polite, throat-clearing cough cut into their conversation.

"Pardon me," Gerald piped up in an exquisitely refined tone. "If I may, whilst neither suggestion constitutes an act which produces a physical byproduct worthy of exhibition, the contextual terms of this particular predicament does, by its very nature, grant more applicable relevance, and therefore credence, towards an act of explicit nature. I *do* think it apt to postulate that such events do indeed touch upon the deepest, most basic fundamental nature of any sexually-reproducing life form; That ineffable, primordial urge which has spirited all movements and efforts and which ultimately has provided the motivations upon which the societies and civilizations in which we now live were initially founded. Yet despite how much we may owe to '*nifty tape measure tricks*', it is hard to beat a good wank."

"Yeah, or a blowjob," Blusoh added.

Alexander stood in silence, incapable of speech.

"Come on," Blusoh continued. "We've got a good opportunity here. Zloykot's checked out, and he's recently been fed. Just give him a quickie, and we can drop you off back at the diner."

"You guys *seriously* want me to come within arm's reach of a drugged-up, jello tiger who can eat people *so easily* that he can do it on *accident*?"

"I just said that he's full!" Blusoh cried. "What's there to worry about?"

Alexander threw his hands up in the air.

"You know what? Fine! Everyone in this universe is crazy, but what the hell? Let's go blow a cannibalistic drug baron while he's high."

"Yeah!" Blusoh shouted enthusiastically. "I mean, technically, there's never been a documented case of a slyger eating another slyger, so the cannibalism bit might be misrepresentative, but we'll let that slide for now. Gerald! You go draw up the paperwork. I'll uh, help get Alexander situated with the boss."

Blusoh and Alexander approached the dais. Zloykot had flopped over onto his back and was staring up at the ceiling. The slyger's bulging stomach dominated their view, but, thankfully, his skin was opaque enough that the contents remained hidden from view.

If it weren't for the comically distended gut, the baron would have looked like quite an impressive body builder. Alexander couldn't help but wonder whether he worked out or was just shaped that way.

Blusoh quietly twisted shut a valve on the hookah and turned to whisper into the baron's ear.

"Psst! Hey Boss? How you doing?"

The slyger gave a lazy blink, but otherwise, he didn't seem to register the question in any meaningful way.

"We're uh... working out a little contract deal here. Just relax and don't worry about anything, all right?"

Blusoh stared in vain for some kind of response for a few seconds before turning back to Alexander.

"Yeah, he's out of it all right," the weasel remarked. "You want me to move him at all for you?"

"Um... No, I think I'm good. I didn't notice he wasn't wearing anything but a blanket."

"Yeah, he's got a love/hate relationship with clothes."

Blusoh pulled back what little blanket was covering the baron to reveal the slyger's ████████ {ANGST}. Zloykot's █████ {ACRIMONY} had several odd little ridges and features in contrast to the generally smooth, toned nature of the rest of him. It wasn't that big compared to his overall proportions, but the alien was significantly larger than Alexander was. Eyeballing it, he estimated that Zloykot's █████ {CHARISMA} was about as thick as a bratwurst, including the bun, and about as long as his forearm.

"I don't know if I can fit that in my mouth," was the sentence Alexander couldn't believe he was saying out loud.

"Well, Gerald's already got the details down in the contract for a blowjob," Blusoh replied. "It doesn't have to be a good one, but you should at least give it a shot."

Alexander took a deep breath, swallowed whatever was left of his pride, and knelt down next to the chaise lounge. Cautiously, he reached out and touched one of the alien's thighs, keeping his attention trained to gauge the alien's reaction. Zloykot didn't stir, but his eyelids lazily drifted up and down with his breathing.

Touching the slyger was a strange experience. His skin was smooth and slightly sticky, while his flesh jiggled oddly due to his lack of bones. Despite himself, Alexander gave a few exploratory pokes and determined that some parts were definitely more firm than others, but all of it seemed rather wobbly.

"Is this guy even able to stand upright?" Alexander asked Blusoh.

"Not at the moment, of course," he replied. "The drugs soften him up in more ways than one. But when he's sober, he can firm up hard enough to hammer nails into the wall. Let me tell you, that makes for a pretty impressive intimidation routine to pound a couple forty-nine-bob nails into a counter with your forehead."

Turning back to the action, reached over and came to grips with Zloykot's ████ {DICHOTOMY}. Gingerly he slid a few strokes up and down, which seemed to get the slyger's attention as he perked right up. The corners of the Baron's mouth drew up into a funny little smile, and his eyes meandered up behind his lids as he grew hard. Smig thanked his lucky stars that the Baron seemed to be a shower, not a grower.

Reluctantly, he gave Zloykot a lick. Smig was surprised to find that the Baron had a surprisingly food-like flavor. Definitely dominated by a tangy flavor like orange marmalade, but with an odd sweet-and-spiced note like honey and cinnamon. Whatever it was, Alexander took it as kind of a mixed blessing that it didn't taste awful. He gave the ███ {HERESY} a couple of licks, acclimating himself while still slowly stroking the ████ {PARADOX} with his hands.

'Out of all the things I missed out on in college,' He thought to himself. "*experimenting with dudes*' was not something I thought I'd miss having experience in, but here I am.'

Bending down a bit lower, Alexander had a go at taking the alien's ████ {RHETORIC} into his mouth. It was awkward, but he was just about able to fit his mouth around it without choking. The slyger took a deep breath and shifted a little, but Alexander wasn't in any position to see much aside from the alien's ██████ {SLANDER} at the moment, so he just carried on and hoped for the best.

Alexander wormed his tongue around Zloykot's ███ {STIG-MA} for a minute. Then, sucking gently, he carefully started taking in as much of the alien's █████ {TIRADE} as he could without activating his gag reflex. Luckily, the slyger's ████ {PROPRIETY} was quite malleable, and the bloopy 'flesh' seemed to shrink slightly to accommodate its confines. Drawing further in, Alexander confirmed that going all the way to the baron's base was far beyond his capabilities, to say nothing of whatever shreds of dignity he might have. Taking a slurpy gulp for effect, he pulled off to catch his breath.

Zloykot was apparently enjoying the experience very much, as a goofy grin had taken over his face. In addition, his reddened eyes were significantly less intimidating now that they were crossed. Somewhat encouraged by this, Alexander went back down for another round. Taking the baron's ████ {MALAISE} back into his mouth, he plunged down and came back up a couple times in even, measured strokes. Concentrating on getting the drug lord off quickly, he tried to pull off swallowing at the apex of each pass.

'God, this is weird,' Smig thought. "Why didn't I just bluff and threaten to call Chancellor Bullfrog or whatever his name wa-"

Alexander's thoughts were interrupted by two heavy, wiggly paws suddenly clamping onto either side of his head. Without warning, he was pulled all the way down the Baron's ████ {MILIEU} until his face was smooshed right into the slyger's squishy abdomen. The impact was brief, as Zloykot immediately let Smig back up, only to pull him back down again, bouncing him against his elastic flesh. Alexander fought against choking as his eyes watered up. He barely heard someone shouting, muffled by the thick, gooey paws clamped firmly over his ears, but the words were drowned out by the shlurpy slapping of his own face against the alien's crotch.

Smig was starting to see stars before his eyes when Zloykot slowed his pounding. He started to panic as he wondered if slyger was about ready to ███ {MALINGER} and whether or not there was anything he could do about it. As it turned out, he didn't have time to react before Zloykot's █████ {HARBINGER} tensed up like a fire hose and ███████ {PONTIFICATED}. The good news was that the slyger hadn't tried to shove him all the way down for the grand finale. The bad news was that he definitely wasn't letting Smig pull away from the massive ▉▉▉▉▉ *{FREUDIAN SLIP}* that had caught him by surprise.

Zloykot grunted as he ▉▉▉▉ *{EXCULPATED}* thick shots of ▉▉▉ *{ENNUI}* that seemed to have the sticky consistency of molasses and an overwhelmingly strong flavor. Sour orange peel came immediately to mind, but it was so much more than that. Trying frantically not to choke or throw up, Alexander's reflexes opted for the lesser evil and forced him to swallow. He could feel Zloykot's hot ▉▉▉ *{SYCOPHANT}* coat his throat and slide down into his stomach. The slyger's warm ▉▉▉▉ *{BOMBAST}* pulsed as it spurted more and more thick liquid straight into poor Smig's throat.

After what felt like an eternity, Alexander felt Blusoh's hands prying in between his head and Zloykot's massive paws. He was finally pulled away, but not before enduring two more shots of the slyger's ▉▉▉▉▉ *{FAIT ACCOPMLI}*. Released from the alien's grasp, Alexander fell backwards onto the floor, gasping for breath, while the baron's ▉▉▉▉▉ *{HEDONISM}* continued to fire off unabated.

"Oh, jeez. You okay, kid?" Blusoh asked. "Did you swallow any of that?"

"Ugh," Alexander coughed and spat out a bubble of slime. "A bit, yeah."

"Ooh. I hope that's not going to be a problem."

"What do you... mean?"

Alexander was starting to feel a little strange. At first, it felt like he was going to throw up, but that rapidly subsided as a mild numbness spread out from his core.

"I should have asked before," Blusoh said, propping him up. "Do you have any drug or chemical allergies?"

"Uh... I don't think so?" Alexander replied. His head was starting to fog up a bit.

"Okay, that's good. Uh... Listen, Alexander, you've done a great job! Let's stand up and get that contract signed, quick."

Throwing his hands under Alexander's arms, Blusoh did his best to hoist him onto his feet. Alexander managed to get upright, but everything started to feel numb and wobbly. His legs shook, and he leaned into the skinny alien to keep from toppling over.

"Am I getting... a fucking contact high?" Alexander asked disbelievingly.

"Well, if you want to split hairs, I think you'd call it secondhand ██████ *{STOICISM}*. Come on, pal. Let's get you over here, quick!"

Blusoh was now trying to get Alexander to walk with one hand over his shoulder, but Alexander's limbs were just not feeling like cooperating anymore.

'Now *this* is something I have experience in, thanks to college,' Smig thought. 'Just have to fall to the side and not break my nose.'

His head was starting to go from tingly to groggy now as he slowly tipped ever further towards the floor in front of him.

"Hey, Blusoh. I think I might-"

Chapter 10
The Brunch

{EDITORIAL NOTE: Due to the sudden and dramatic drop off of readership in the last section, The Board of B.A.S.T.A.R.D.S. has regretfully been forced to sack former Chief Klerman Dwahoogaloo. Redactions have once again been placed in the trusted hands of Sir Hucklebourn, on the provision that his work will not cause 5/6ths of the readership to fall asleep or leave to look for a dictionary.}

Alexander woke up. Every part of his body felt dead and opening his bleary eyes only revealed an extremely close-up view of his left arm resting on a hard surface. Slowly he raised his head, blinking in the light, to reveal a wobbly view of the Intergalactic Grotto of Waffles. Something tickled his neck, and he wearily grabbed at the spot. Paper crinkled next to his ear, and Alexander found the culprit was a hastily scribbled note which read:

Sorry again for the screw-up, pal. Left a copy of the contract in your pocket with a little extra something (call it a tip). Good job sucking off the boss.

Wow, that sounded better in my head.

-Blusoh and Gerald, D.D.S.

Alexander squinted at the paper for a while before recollection finally swam through the swamp of his mind to reach the forefront of his thought.

"Ugh," he slurred, now painfully aware of where the godawful, rotten orange taste in his mouth had come from.

Alexander let the note fall from his hand onto the table and swiveled his head to look around. He'd been stuffed into a booth in the far corner of the restaurant. Shifting his weight from one elbow to the other, he reached down to pull out the crumpled contract and a voucher for a free meal that Zloykot's goons had hastily stuffed into his pocket. He stared blankly at them for a moment as his stomach shifted around uneasily. Food was about the last thing on his mind in this exact moment, but he could definitely go for something to wash out his mouth.

From the look of things, service at the IGOW didn't seem to penetrate any further out than the handful of booths right next to the front counter, so Smig reluctantly made a groggy effort to hoist himself up on his feet and stumble over to an empty stool at the end of the counter. He had barely collapsed into the seat and cradled his head in his hands when Wyrmbs slapped an overflowing glass of ice water and a menu down in front of him.

"Thanks," Alexander managed to croak.

"Somethin' to eat?" Wyrmbs asked with her characteristic lack of enthusiasm.

"Uh, yeah, sure," he said, just wanting an excuse for more water.

"Same you had last time?"

"Sure."

"Archibald!" Wyrmbs yelled as she hustled down the line. "I need a 36. No bean. No beef!"

Alexander sipped at the water, washing out the sick taste in his mouth before taking a few gulps to rehydrate. Gradually the vague threat of a headache died down, and he was left with just a mild but persistent queasiness. Settling himself in, Smig's ear involuntarily tuned in to the conversation being shouted back and forth down the counter to his right.

"- I thought the Bodgers of Rhygon 2 bought out the contract rights!" a gruff alien called down the bar. "How'd you wind up in construction?"

"Beats me!" a female voice shouted back. "Like I was telling Yarlick over here, I wasn't even trying to get into the job. I signed up for that damn fast-track program, and it screwed up my application!"

"What *were* you trying to get into?"

"Well, I dunno if I want to say," she said.

"Why not? Were you aiming to be a marketing director?"

"Watch your language!" Wyrms shouted from the back.

"God no!" the female voice replied. "I've got more dignity than that! I was trying to apply to be a concubine."

Alexander's eyebrows raised in surprise. He shifted and glanced down the bar, trying to discern if he'd heard correctly. Unfortunately, whoever was talking was lost in the general cacophony among the crowd of aliens milling around the counter.

"Ho, ho ho!" a voice chortled over the noise. "Now, what would you want to be one of them for?"

"Now, hear me out!" the lady called back. "Listen, I figured it would be an easy gig, you know? Get some decent pay without having to do a whole lot of actual work. Fooling around with some rich dude on the weekends doesn't sound so bad at the rates they were offering. So you can imagine my confusion when I showed up for first-day training, and they handed me the high-vis jacket and a hardhat."

"Why'd you keep going, then?"

"Honestly, it took me a lot longer than it should have to work out that I wasn't being trained up for some crazy kink shit. Then by that time, I figured out that construction was just what I was looking for! I'm getting paid almost twice as much to stack orange cones and hang around job sites for days on end while the corporate bureaucracies wrangle with the government bureaucracies."

"Sure has the same amount of people fucking each other over!" Someone called out.

A hearty laugh rippled across the diner. Alexander gave up trying to see past the rowdy crowd and slumped back to the countertop, contemplating the weird coincidence that seemed to be going on. Given that his mental processing speed was only now approaching the speed of smell, he didn't discount the idea that he was still riding the aftershocks of whatever substances had abused him yesterday.

"Order up!" Wyrmbs called out.

Plate, spread rack, and bill appeared on the counter in a flash. Alexander ignored it and took another gulp of water. He was mid-swallow when a piercing whistle cut through the entire restaurant. Luckily, everyone turned around to stare at the source of the disturbance and not at the water Smig had just sprayed down his shirt.

"Aw, shit," he mumbled.

He was busy grabbing some napkins from the dispenser as the whistler approached. The alien was a large fellow who could best be described as a cross between a four-armed marmot and a red Tyrannosaurus Rex. He wore a militaristic uniform and had some kind of menacing sidearm holstered on his belt. Flanking either side of him were two similarly built and outfitted junior officers, one green and one orange.

"I'm looking for an Alexander Smig!" the intimidating figure called out.

Smig jumped a little in surprise, accidentally dropping a damp napkin. He had no idea who these guys were, but it probably wasn't a good thing that they were after him.

"It's pronounced *Alexandra Smick*, ya big galoot!" the lady's voice called out.

"Oh, not you, Alexandra," the four-armed officer replied. "Didn't know you were in here. I'm actually looking for an *Alexander Smig*. Supposed to be male."

"Oh, that's a weird coincidence."

"You're telling me!"

Alexander fumbled with his napkins and looked around. His head swam vaguely for some kind of plan, but nothing cohesive was rising above the muggy swamp at the moment. Standing up to leave would probably draw too much attention. The officer called out again.

"Well, if no one's heard of this guy, Big Chuck asked me to tell y'all he wants crew 20B-1 to head out and meet him at the southern polar parkade."

There was a general murmur as most of the patrons began to shuffle around, slapping cash on the counter. Alexander dug around in his pockets. Maybe he could slip out unnoticed in the crowd.

"If I can ask you to go single file, that'd help me ensure this Smig fellow isn't trying to slip out unnoticed in the crowd."

Smig swore silently as the patrons complied. As they began to filter out, he frantically considered his options. His stomach gurgled and reminded him he was in no condition to attempt a mad dash without a dramatic, attention-grabbing expulsion of its contents. Glancing around, Smig's eyes happened to fall on the lady who must have been speaking earlier. It was a little strange to see another human in the midst of a bunch of aliens, and he stared as she made her way out of the cafe.

"You!" the officer barked, pointing at Alexander and snapping him out of a daze. "Yeah, you on the end! Are you Alexander Smig?"

"Um, well i-"

The officers stomped over to the bar and now towered right over Alexander.

"You're a Yearthling, right?" the alien asked.

"Uh... I'm an Earthling," Alexander offered uneasily.

"Then you might not know that it's a *crime* to lie to a Federal officer. Is your name Alexander Smig?"

"Is it a crime to not tell you?"

"No, but if you refuse, you'll need to be taken in to fill out form F-451: Withholding of Identifying Metrics and Personal Stuff. Only 46 pages."

"Oh Christ," he gulped. "Yeah, I'm Alexander Smig."

The officers glanced at each other and took up positions on either side. The big red one cleared his throat and addressed him directly.

"I am Captain Yha-Bihgg Galoot, in the service of the Varangitorian guard of Bulbeeyoog, Chancellor of the Federation of Everything. Your presence has been requested, Mr. Smig."

"It has?" Alexander asked rather timidly.

"Yes, and we are here to escort you to your destination."

"Oh, jeez. You guys sure you're not professional kidnappers?"

"Afraid not. Please come with us."

Captain Galoot's tone brokered no argument, and neither did the unyielding grip of his under-officers as they lifted Alexander off the stool and onto his feet.

"Hey, uh, I should pay my bill first, right?" Alexander stammered.

"Don't bother," the Captain growled. "Put it on the victualer tab, Wyrmbs. I'll be in tomorrow."

Wyrmbs gave an incoherent grumble as the officers manhandled Smig out the door and across the mall. Alexander made a valiant effort not to stumble or stagger too much as he tried to keep pace with the Captain's march.

"Uh, can I ask why I'm being brought in?" He asked.

"That's between you and the Chancellor." Galoot replied bluntly.

Smig was sure that this wasn't a good sign, but at this point, trying anything desperate would probably have just ended with him throwing up on his handlers, which probably would not improve their disposition. After a brisk walk, they came up to a private docking entrance guarded by two more aliens in uniforms similar to the Captain's.

"Four entrants, two to embark!" Galoot called out.

"Acknowledged!" one of them replied with a smart salute. "Four to enter, two passengers to embark. You are free to enter, Captain Galoot!"

The Captain returned their salutes as the entry gate swung open just long enough for them to pass through. On the other side was a large room that looked like the security circus at an airport. They approached a stiff-backed alien in a blue uniform seated at a small lectern. Said individual stared them down with at least four or five eyeballs and an electronic barcode scanner.

"Papers, please," the stiff-backed alien murmured in monotone.

Captain Galoot handed over a passport booklet that expanded into an impossibly long punch sheet. The desk guard glanced it over before scanning it, affixing several stamps, and punching a few oddly shaped holes in strategic locations. This he returned to the Captain, who began trying to work the myriad of folds back into some kind of compact shape.

"Are you the only passenger?" the attendant inquired.

"Him too." Galoot thumbed towards Alexander.

"Papers," the attendant said, pointing a few disinterested eyeballs at Smig.

Lacking his wallet and any better ideas, Alexander pulled out the temporary employment ID that Grand Master Whoople had given him and passed it along. The security guard scanned it and then pressed the card against a glass surface, causing a series of clicks and beeps to emanate from the lectern.

"Are either of you carrying anything liquid, fragile, or perishable?" he asked.

"No," Captain Galoot replied.

"Uh, no," Alexander said, trying not to burp up something foul.

"Any containers or vessels pressurized over 13 cubits of mercury?"

"No," Captain Galoot replied.

"I... don't think so?" Alexander said.

"Do you have on your person any permits, passes, contracts, writs, warrants, subpoenas, citations, licenses, written agreements, or other concordances, formal or informal, that have been committed to writing?"

"12 subpoena rounds for my service pistol," Captain Galoot replied.

"That's fine, Captain," The guard said. "What about you?"

"Uh, well, I do have one contract."

"Please remove any paperwork you have and place it in the bin, sir."

Alexander complied, placing the still unsigned blowjob contract in a grey bin.

"All right," the guard said. "Please step up to the analyzer."

The officers herded Smig onto a yellow boundary box marked on the floor. Before them loomed the entrance to a claustrophobic, full-body scanning device. Another security attendant in blue approached them.

"All right, one at a time," the attendant stated. "Please step into the analyzer."

The officers released their hold on Alexander as Galoot nudged him forward. Shakily, he clambered through the narrow entrance into the analyzer.

"Please hold your upper torso limbs above the center of your mass," the attendant said, raising his three arms above his combination torso-head as an example.

Smig lifted his arms. A loud buzzing noise enveloped him as a robotic arm swept around in a circle. A buzzer sounded off somewhere outside the contraption.

"Sir, do you have any controlled substances on your person?" the attendant asked.

"Uh, no?" Alexander replied, suddenly mindful of a slick remnant of that awful taste in the back of his mouth. "Dumb question. What counts as a substance?"

The attendant sighed.

"Please step out of the analyzer and come this way," the alien ordered.

Alexander emerged and was led off to the side. The attendant motioned towards a red circle marked on the floor.

"Please stand in the center of the annulus."

As Alexander complied, another alien came up with a small cage containing some sort of creature that looked an awful lot like a tiny iridescent elephant. It seemed to scrutinize him with the most disconcertingly suspicious eye he'd ever seen on an animal.

"Please hold your upper torso limbs straight out on either side," the attendant instructed.

Alexander complied, trying to avoid the tiny elephant's squinting glare as the guard held its cage up so it could literally sniff him out. As its nose meandered around, Alexander swore he could hear the thing muttering some kind of incomprehensible curses under its breath before suddenly exploding into a minuscule little sneeze. It would have been the most adorable thing in the world had the little quasi-elephant not aimed it directly at his face. The attendant pulled the cage back, and the elephant whispered something that sounded excessively judgmental into his ear.

"Are you carrying any saffronated-absinthene on your person?" The attendant asked.

"Oh jeez," Alexander replied. "Maybe? I don't know. Look, I wound up in a weird situation where I was asked to-"

"Hold on a moment," the attendant interrupted, retreating back behind a barrier to confer quietly with the other security attendant. After a moment, he turned back to Alexander.

"Please remain still. We need to do a pass with the drug-sniffing bees."

"The what?"

Alexander's question had come too late. A massive swarm of alien bees had already descended from somewhere above and had now enveloped him.

"Again, please don't move!" the attendant called out above the thunderous buzzing. "And try not to scream so much. It distracts them, which prolongs the process."

At length, the bees disappeared just as quickly as they had come, leaving Alexander with distressed hair and a spike in his heart rate. The deafening buzz had been replaced by the soft, raspy snickering of the little elephant creature in its cage as the security attendants quietly observed the readout from a monitor.

"Hmm, very light readings," the attendant said. "Looks like it's mixed in with a whole lot of... oh."

He turned to face Alexander.

"Have you been, um... *intimately involved* with anyone under the influence recently? Possibly a slyger?"

"Yes," Alexander gasped, now only hoping to get past this whole ordeal.

"Okay, you've got some er... *residue* in your system from that, then. That's not going to be a problem today, but in the future, we'd appreciate it if you could declare that up front at the check-in desk. It'd save us all some trouble."

"You're telling me."

The security attendant ushered him back to Captain Galoot, who was in the middle of putting his boots back on. He didn't ask what the problem had been, and Alexander certainly was not inclined to offer an explanation. The under officers had disappeared, leaving the Captain to march off with a hand on Smig's shoulder. As they came up to the exit portal, another attendant held out Alexander's contract, which had been sealed in some kind of clear plastic.

"Here you are, sir," the attendant said. "Please do not unseal the container until after you have disembarked at your destination."

Galoot slowed his pace just long enough for Alexander to grab the bag. Once out of the security zone, they marched down a few long corridors with indecipherable destination markers until they arrived at a strangle little alcove. A bored-looking blob of an alien sat at a desk with a small tabletop console set askew on top. Alexander didn't get much of a look at him or her as the Captain hurriedly shuffled into the room, but he'd never seen anyone with a circular, donut-like torso before. He wasn't sure what kept the necktie on, but it sure drew the eye the way it dangled down in front of the hole in its chest.

"Two for telephacsimilation!" Galoot barked out. "Op order: FDMF Mahogany."

"Mm-hmm," the other alien hummed without looking up.

The Captain positioned himself and Alexander to one side of the desk, directly in front of a strange little tube sticking out of the console.

"Don't move," Galoot growled.

The bored alien swiped a limb across a glass control plate, and a photographic click sounded out from the console. They stood there for a long moment. Alexander was just starting to wonder if he should say anything when the desk attendant shifted again.

"Got it," it said noncommittally.

Captain Galoot heaved a sigh, and his shoulders sagged a little as he relaxed.

"Well, looks like early retirement for us, huh?" he said in a suddenly amicable tone.

"What?" Alexander asked, confused.

"Haven't you ever done a telephacsimile before?" Galoot asked.

"No, I've never even heard of it."

"Oh. Well, have you heard of teleportation?"

"Sure. Something that can beam you from one place to another?"

"It's kind of like that, except that the process of teleporting a physical thing from one place to another just isn't practical on an economic scale. Telephacsimile is the next best thing. It basically copies all of your information as nonphysical data and sends that out to the other end, where they use it to print a new copy of you filled up with all of your thoughts and memories from before."

"Huh... I think I've heard something like that before on some sci-fi movie, but, I think, in that one, the originals got destroyed in the process."

"Good grief! Nobody would be crazy enough to use one if *that* was true! No sir, we get to retire and move out to a special resort world set up purely for the use of telephacsimile originals, while the new copies of us have to move on with our old lives."

"Huh. That doesn't sound so bad."

"I know, right? Only drawback is the retirement upkeep gets expensive incredibly fast, so the whole system is pretty heavily restricted. Usually, it's reserved for extremely important business or people who are willing to shell out a stupid amount of cash. Lucky for us, this is a government trip. We don't pay a single bob outside the mimeography tax."

"Wow. So, that's it? Where were you even taking me? I mean, where did you send... other me?"

"Well, for security reasons, all I can say is apparently you were in line for a direct audience with the Chancellor himself. No clue what for, but in my experience, it's damn lucky he wanted you there as quickly as possible. Lucky for you here, of course. Definitely not for the copy that's going to go see him right now. There's not many reasons the Chancellor would want to schedule a personal audience so quickly, but..."

Galoot trailed off, staring at the far wall.

"Pad's gotta clear," the donut said. "Next departure is en route."

"Oop, come on," the Captain replied, stepping down. "I'll walk ya down to the shuttle."

Alexander followed the Captain down the hall. The whole thing was perplexing, but it sounded like he might have dodged one hell of a bullet, so he figured he shouldn't ask too many questions. Not about the Chancellor, at least. He still had plenty of other concerns.

"So..." he said thoughtfully. "Aren't there, like, ethical concerns about making copies of people?"

"Like what?" Galoot asked.

"I don't know. I guess it just seems like the sort of thing where that would come up. Does the uh, other copy of me know that this happened?"

"Well, that's a thing. If you didn't know anything about tele-phacsimilation before the data copy was made, he'll have no idea. Honestly, if you want my advice, I'd say don't think on it too hard and just enjoy the free early retirement."

Alexander thought that over as they wandered into a transport depot that looked for all the world like an elaborate subway station.

"Hey, Captain?" he asked. "Could I ask you something?"

"You can call me Yha-Bihgg. What's on your mind?"

"Is there any chance I could run into that copy of me in the future?"

"In all likelihood, no. The odds of bumping into them at random are slim to none. I mean, still better odds than winning the multiversal lottery, but that's not saying much. Why do you ask?"

"I don't know. The concept just kinda weirds me out a little."

"Well, I wouldn't worry about it. Like I said, even if that audience with the Chancellor does turn out to be a friendly chat, the statistical odds mean it's practically impossible."

"Like bumping into a random meteoroid in a small spaceship out in open space?" Alexander asked.

"Exactly!" Galoot exclaimed.

Chapter 11
His Esteemed Excellency Bulbeeyoog, Chancellor of the Federation of Everything and Protector of Its Citizen's Rights, Liberties, and Dental Benefits

Alexander felt very strange, almost like he had been very rapidly woven together in the space of an instant halfway through the click of the tabletop console. His head spun a little more than it had been as he blinked and looked around. The entire room had suddenly changed from the strange little alcove to an open observation deck. Large windows revealed a sweeping, dramatic view of space.

"Damn," Captain Galoot muttered under his breath. "Lucky sons of guns. You must be pretty important to warrant a telephacsimile ."

"What?" Alexander asked, still somewhat disoriented.

"Never mind. Come along."

The Captain marched off, with Alexander stumbling behind him as quickly as he could manage. Moving from the observation deck, they passed through a series of corridors until they came to a large antechamber. Several guards with impressively elaborate uniforms and brightly colored head tentacles stood rigidly at strategic points around the room. Captain Galoot came to attention in front of one in even finer dress who was standing next to a small desk that seemed to be fabricated from something like hardened wool. The guard somehow straightened up even more than he had been and fixed the two of them with a firm gaze.

"Colonel Ayekant Behlee Viits Notbuth-Ar of the 18th Federal Dragoon Corps Honor Guard presiding. State your name, rank, and business."

"Captain Yha-Bihgg Galoot, 91st Varangitorian Regiment, with Alexander Smig, Federal Civilian. I have escorted Mr. Smig here, per the Chancellor's request for his presence."

The Colonel briskly turned to consult a specialized display that blended into the woolwork. After only a few moments of contemplation, he shot his gaze back at them.

"The Chancellor extends his thanks for your service, Captain. You are dismissed."

The Colonel raised his hand to his chin and waggled his fingers in some kind of odd salute. Galoot repeated the gesture.

"If I may, Colonel. Always a pleasure to assist a fellow of the Ancient and Honorary Order of the Woodchucks."

"The pleasure is all mine, Captain," the Colonel replied gracefully.

This done, Captain Galoot did an about-face and marched out of the room, leaving Alexander with a strange parting glance.

"Mr. Smig," the Colonel addressed him. "Do you have any weapons or dangerous items on your person?"

"Uh, all I have is an ID card and this contract."

"May I see them, please."

Alexander pulled them out and set them on the wooly desk. The Colonel leaned over them and scrutinized them with a third eye embedded in his elbow. It was an unusual feature, to begin with, but Smig felt a strange, hollow numbness creep up on him as he stared at it. Abruptly, the Colonel withdrew his arm, and the sensation retreated just as quickly as it came.

"Everything seems in order," the Colonel commented. "If you would accompany me, please."

Stepping out in front of him, the alien led Alexander through the heavy doors at the far end of the room. Marching in, Smig was somewhat surprised to find himself in a sort of office space that seemed far less regal than all of the pomp in the antechamber had led him to expect. There were, of course, impressive views of space through the window-like view screens on either side of the room, but the furnishings were stylishly simple and practical.

The only aspect that made the space truly daunting was the scale of things. There were two massive sofas facing each other that looked like they could comfortably fit five or six people lying down. Between them sat a coffee table that was almost as tall as Alexander and could hold a banquet feast fit for any king. Beyond these was a desk that towered above everything else in the room since this had been specially made to stand comfortably within the Chancellor's physically dominating reach.

Whatever lay beyond that was obscured by the angle, but Smig could see twin wisps of smoke rising up to the living popcorn ceiling. The little kernels appeared to be congregating around and consuming the smoke.

"Mister Chancellor, Mr. Alexander Smig is here to see you," the Colonel called out from the threshold.

"Very good, Colonel," an impossibly deep, grainy voice called out from the far end of the room. "Please show him in."

The Colonel fixated Alexander with a piercing stare and brought a hand up to rest on the hilt of his ceremonial flammard.

"Follow me, and make no trouble," the Colonel said quietly.

Alexander was pretty nervous, given the intimidating surroundings, but the prospect of potentially getting skewered if he stepped out of line was enough to get him moving. He followed timidly as the Colonel led him up to a platform designed to accommodate the disproportion in scale between the Chancellor and his visitors. Coming to a halt, the Colonel activated a control, which caused the platform to slowly rise up before the desk, so they could come face-to-face with the minister of ministers. Slowly creeping up to the level of the gargantuan desk, a large executive chair came into view, though its high back was turned away to hide its occupant.

"Mister Chancellor," the Colonel announced. "May I present to you Mr. Alexander Smig."

The ludicrously oversized chair swiveled around to reveal the body of an immense, dragon-like creature dressed in an eight-piece suit. To Smig's surprise, however, it did not reveal the Chancellor's face, as this was still obscured by a pixelated effect exactly as it had appeared before him via telepholographic projection.

"Thank you, Colonel," the Chancellor said in his deep, growling voice. "You may return to your post. Please see that the proceedings are not interrupted."

Colonel Notbuth-Ar saluted and backed onto a separate section of the platform, which lowered him back down to the floor. Alexander was sweating and had no idea what was in store for him as he spent an eternity listening to the Colonel's boots marching all the way back to the entry. Finally, the doors swung shut behind the officer, and grim silence deafened the room as the Chancellor seemed to scrutinize him.

The monstrous alien sat calmly with his hands resting on the desk in front of him, yet Smig could feel an uncomfortably hot breeze that was, to his mind, undoubtedly breath that could turn to fire and roast him in an instant. The only thing in the room that was moving was the popcorn ceiling casually milling around the tendrils of smoke.

"Well, I'm glad to finally meet you in person, Alexander Smig," the Chancellor opened with a disarmingly casual tone. "Do you prefer to go by anything in particular?"

"Oh, uh. Well um... Alexander is fine," he replied, somewhat caught off guard by the question.

"Nervous?" the draconic alien chuckled, and Alexander swore he saw a wisp of smoke rise out of the shimmering pixels.

"Um, a little, yes. if I'm honest, Mr. Chancellor, sir, the last few days have been a he- uh, they've been a challenge."

"Don't worry about any formalities, Alexander. Do you mind if I ask you a few questions?"

"No, not at all," Smig lied.

The Chancellor leaned back and seemed to inspect the claws on one hand. The exquisitely crafted executive chair did not creak, but Alexander swore he could still feel the immense weight being shifted around. Perhaps the alien's casual demeanor meant that he wasn't quite angry with him, but that only left Smig with the equally worrying possibility that the Chancellor would seriously expect him to perform some actual concubine-ly duties.

"What kind of work did you do in construction before Earth joined the Federation?"

"Oh," Alexander stammered, again distracted by the character of the question. "Well, mostly just general labor and equipment operation. I usually ended up driving the backhoes and bulldozers."

"Work on any interesting projects?"

"Uh... well, some larger stuff like office buildings and apartments, but nothing terribly spectacular. I guess there was that demo at the Great Mall a few years ago. Used to be the biggest mall in Kansas, I think."

The Chancellor idly tapped at a console-like surface on his desk that was angled away from Alexander. His body language seemed to imply that he wasn't quite paying attention, but from what Alexander could tell through the pixels, the alien's head hadn't moved. Smig couldn't shake that same feeling of being watched by unseen eyes that he had experienced in the interview room.

"Do you have the ID card that Grand Master Whoople gave you?" the Chancellor asked abruptly.

"Yeah," Alexander said, trying not to jump. "I've got it right here. Do you need it?"

"No, and *you* don't need it anymore either. I have to apologize, Alexander. Security is of chief concern in my line of work, and it took a little time for the analyzers to decide that you're not an impostor or some other kind of threat. Thankfully, they've run your info through, and everything checks out."

Smig started to breathe a little easier.

"Earth's still new in the system," the Chancellor continued. "So it took a bit longer than usual to back-check all of your data. As of now, you are registered and should be listed in the system here and everywhere else in the Federation. One of the perks of being a registered Federal employee is that you don't need to worry about presenting ID."

"Ah. Well, that's great. So... I'm an employee?"

"That's right. Though I have to say you made more than a few of my advisors jump out of their skins when you took off with a professional kidnapper as soon as you got your temporary ID card."

Alexander immediately lost any relief that he'd had and tensed up.

"You heard about that?" he asked nervously.

"Saw the whole sequence myself on the security tapes."

The Chancellor leaned forward and crossed his fingers in his hands, openly displaying his sharp claws at an equal level with the platform Smig was standing on. Alexander could only assume that he had similarly sharp fangs obscured behind the pixels.

"Now, Alexander, you seem reasonably bright, so you can probably imagine the kind of questions a little episode like that might provoke. Some of my people thought you were doing anything from selling the id on the black market, trading it off to an assassin, or... using it to forge documents."

A dim flash of red and a thicker puff of smoke arose from the pixelation as the Chancellor paused before straightening a little.

"They advised me to void your contract and take immediate '*security measures*'... but I was curious. Ryan Schmidtke has run some legally dubious contracts before, but he's never stumbled into anything *that* serious. Just didn't seem like his modus operandi, you know?"

"Yeah," Alexander squeaked. Something in the back of his mind still had the gumption to wonder if Ryan's supposed name change had accomplished anything at all.

"So then, imagine the consternation when the two of you were picked up by agents connected to Baron Zloykot and the Space Mafia."

The red, glowing flicker was now definitely persistent about where the alien's eyes should be. The popcorn kernels above had apparently sensed something; for they now shied away from the smoke and migrated to the far corners of the room. Smig wondered if the platform was high enough up that the fall would kill him.

"As luck would have it, we have some intelligence sources that filled us in on what took place at the Baron's Casbah. Certainly an interesting series of... *happenstances* you were juggled through."

"Honestly, I can hardly believe it myself," Alexander stammered, unsure if he was digging himself deeper or not. "You'd probably think I was nuts if I told you it was all out of my control."

The Chancellor laughed and unfolded his hands but did not lean back in his chair.

"You'd think *I* was nuts if I told you how often I've encountered these kinds of bizarre circumstances. The multiverse is a big place, Alexander, and you wouldn't believe some of the weird strings of nonsense I have to deal with on a daily basis. I've learned that sometimes the best option is to wait and see what falls off the fan and onto the floor. Thirteen out of fourteen times, it turns out to be excrement, but sometimes you catch a glint from the eye of that bastard goblin named luck, and you find solid latinum."

The Chancellor paused, leaning in closer as his burning eyes seemed to stare straight past Alexander's sweat into his soul. Close enough, he could feel the Chancellor's painfully hot breath wash over him.

"So what have I found, Alexander? We know mostly what happened, but the tale is rarely ever unfurled to its fullest extent. I'm willing to believe that there's a reasonable-ish explanation for everything that's taken place in the last few days, but I would like some kind of reassurance directly from you. You don't need to lay out a play-by-play of your whole version of events. Just tell me flat out, Alexander, is there anything *subversive* going on?"

Alexander swallowed a big gulp of air as he answered.

"No, sir," he replied as firmly as he could.

"Do you intend any harm to my person or to the Chancellor-ship?"

"Hell no."

"Do you intend to help or provide aid to anyone else who may do so?"

"Absolutely not."

There was a momentary pause, the Chancellor's eyes burning like hot coals through the pixelation. Suddenly a soft 'boop' noise broke the tension from a hidden speaker somewhere. The Chancellor gave a sigh of relief and sank back in his chair. A thick plume of smoke rose up to the ceiling as the light in his eyes died down.

"Thank you, Clara," The Chancellor said into the intercom on his desk. "Well, Alexander. Looks like you're legit. Thank goodness. I hate people getting vaporized in my office."

"What?" Alexander asked incredulously.

"I'm sorry to have to run you through the mill," the Chancellor apologized, looking at his display. "Again, it's all security procedure. One last triple-check for luck. You managed to score 92% truthful and 86% honest on your lie detector test, which puts the odds of you being a near-perfect robot replica or an *exceptionally* dedicated traveling brush salesman at twenty-nine blobillion to one. Everything's all good for real this time."

The Chancellor flipped a switch, and the pixelation on his face disappeared in a wholly abrupt and underwhelming manner. Already taken aback at the circumstances, Alexander jumped a little at this sudden reveal of Bulbeeyoog's appearance.

"Ah, there we go," Bulbeeyoog said in a noticeably squeakier voice. "That thing gets tiring after a while. You okay there, Alexander?"

Smig stared at the Chancellor with a mixture of shock and confusion. The alien's actual appearance was an entire galaxy apart from the menacing, intimidating aura he had radiated before. Bulbeeyoog was busy removing an odd pair of thin wire glasses that seemed to go over the top of his prescription lenses. They had been glowing when he took them off, but now they were dim, and only a tiny line of smoke wisped off of them as he folded them up and stuffed them in a desk drawer.

"Uh, yeah. I guess I've just never seen a, um... dragon-like person with hair like that before."

"Oh, I tend to forget about that," Bulbeeyoog said thoughtfully. "I suppose most Ploboids do like to stay clean-shaven, but since I've got the pixelation on practically all of the time, I just don't bother. Would you mind if we chat for a bit? I'd like to get to know you a little better now that we've got the security gubbins out of the way."

"Yeah... I mean, as long as everything's all good now," Alexander replied, still a little shaken at the thought that he could have been vaporized, or worse, only mere moments before.

"Everything's fine, Alexander. I'm sorry that got you worked up, but you're now a trusted individual in my eyes. Why don't we have a seat over there where it's more comfortable?"

Bulbeeyoog rose. As he did so, the platform that Alexander was standing on began to gently retract back into the floor. Alexander somewhat shakily followed the Chancellor back to the sofas, which thankfully had steps up to the top, so he didn't need to clamber around in an ungainly manner. He did have to squirm a little to ensure the seat cushion didn't swallow him as the Chancellor sank into place next to him.

"So, um. You're not upset about anything?" Alexander asked, still a little wary.

"What do I have to be upset about?" Bulbeeyoog replied. "You said yourself that you got caught up in a weird string of events, and from what I've seen, I believe it. You've had a hell of a time for someone who wasn't even trying to be a concubine."

The Chancellor chuckled at Alexander's shocked expression.

"You know about that?" Smig asked.

"Yeah, I was pretty sure of that even before I read through your employment history. Grand Master Whoople puts on a good show, but when you deal with as many *political relationships* as I do on a daily basis, you can spot an amateur a couple light-yelaageroos away. I don't mean to insult you, Alexander, but if I fully intended to hire someone based on their sexual performance, I have no shortage of options. Not to mention that you *are* a little small compared to me."

"No kidding," Alexander replied, with an internal sigh of relief. "So why *did* you hire me?"

"Well, not only did I catch certain comments that were append-ed alongside your application forms, I happened to be in a position to overhear some of your conversation with Whoople concerning the mix-up before the interview started. And, well... this may sound a little silly to you, Alexander, but I've never once come across another person who seems to share my feelings on how tremendously tedious and awful paperwork can be."

Alexander was somewhat taken aback.

"Are you serious?" Alexander asked.

"Absolutely!" the Chancellor exclaimed. "I can't stand it! Can you imagine being stuck in a job doing nothing but paperwork for yelaageroos on end? There isn't a waking moment that goes by where I'm not drowning in it!"

"Huh, I would have thought that being the big boss would mean you could delegate most of that."

"You'd think so, wouldn't you?" Bulbeeyoog sighed. "But let me tell you, Alexander. Everyone in the Federation is *crazy*! It's considered a badge of honor to have a high volume of paperwork. Nobody seems to get what an absolute pain in the narbles it is. Everyone I've ever opened up to just gives me funny looks like I'm complaining about having too much air to breathe. It's the worst!"

"Wow. Don't you have any way out of it? I mean, if you hate it as much as I do, I'd seriously consider resigning if I couldn't get someone else to do it."

"No Chancellor has *ever* resigned in the entire history of the Federation. It's sort of possible in *theory*, but you know what I'd need to do to make that happen?"

"What?"

"Reconvene the Federal Parliament and ask it to draft an amendment to the Grand Charter. Now we're not just talking about paperwork but committees, hearings, sittings, smellings, debates, and virtual mountains of forms for every little step of the process."

"Holy shit!" Alexander exclaimed. "How long are you in office for?"

Bulbeeyoog gave a long, drawn-out sigh and slumped down further into the couch.

"Do you want the whole spiel?" He asked.

"Well, you hired me because I can sympathize, right? As far as I'm concerned, you can fire away. I've done my fair share of sitting on the clock and listening to the boss gripe."

"All right," the Chancellor chuckled a little before taking a deep breath.

Chapter 12
The Move In

Alexander wasn't sure how long he had been in Chancellor Bulbeeyoog's office, but it had to have been hours. During that time, Bulbeeyoog had not only given him far more detail about the Federal Government than he'd ever wanted to know but had *somehow* convinced Alexander to let him rest his refrigerator-sized head in his lap and even have him attempt to braid his hair. Poor Alexander had never braided hair before (and it showed), but Bulbeeyoog assured him that he just enjoyed the sensation. It was a lucky thing the couch was especially forgiving; otherwise, Alexander's legs would have been purple by this point.

"So let me get this straight," Alexander said, fiddling with a clump of hair in a way he hoped was suitably stimulating. "You get appointed by the parliament to be a candidate for Chancellor, along with, like, five other guys. Then the general public votes for which candidate they want to elect, and they voted for you. After that, there was something about a blessing?"

"You need to be granted the assent of the Grand Poobah of all that can be surveyed, Herman Nematode," the Chancellor replied.

"Right, but he's been dead for however long."

"6.9 million yelaageroos."

"Yeah, so that's largely ceremonial at this point?"

"Pretty much," Bulbeeyoog shrugged.

"Anyways, after all that, you get one term as Chancellor before the next election. But for unrelated reasons, you ended up dismissing parliament halfway into your term, so they can't appoint any new candidates to hold another election. You *could* reconvene them to do that, but they'd have to catch up on the back catalog of tabled legislature before getting on to new business."

"Yes, and it's been somewhere between forty and fifty thousand yelaageroos since I dismissed them."

"And we figured that was somewhere around two thousand Earth years, right?"

"I think so."

"So why did you dismiss them in the first place?" Alexander asked.

"Well, I didn't *want* to do it. I was forced into it. You see, under the terms of the Federal Charter, there's no provision for allowing the members of Parliament to take any kind of break while in session. They're just supposed to continue working until the session ends. Inevitably, of course, it doesn't take long before an 8/9ths majority of them need to use the bathroom. *That* is the minimum required to issue a Federal Mandate to the Chancellor, which is basically an ultimatum where I either have to do exactly what parliament says or else dissolve the parliament and call for a general election."

"So, either you let them use the bathroom, or you dismiss them and elect a whole new legislative body? That sounds insane."

"It's even crazier because it's not *dismissal*. That second option is *dissolution*. Literally, flood the chambers with a potent mixture of super strong bases to dissolve parliament. That tends to make the next parliament assembly a tad skittish, so no Chancellor has ever done it since Ignill Hooper did so accidentally back in 17,485,921. They've made the label on the switch for that, much easier to read since then, in case you were wondering."

"Why is that even an option?" Alexander asked incredulously.

"Honestly, even *I'm* not sure about that, and I majored in political history. Anyways, getting 8/9ths of that lot to agree on anything is so rare that I naturally figured a brief dismissal of parliament would be the lesser evil compared to the headache of organizing a full-blown general election, so I opted for that. What I didn't realize at the time was that the wily bastards weren't just after the restroom this time. They had figured out a way to get an extended, paid vacation by *asking* for a standard bathroom break but then leaving some of their cronies behind to hit the courtesy button that grants them a few more milli-yelaageroos onto their time to finish washing their hands."

"What, like a snooze button?"

"Exactly! They've been continuously hitting that damn button ever since, and there's no sign they're going to let up anytime in the foreseeable future. The only way I can get them to reconvene *legally* is if they manage to flub up the button pushing and their time runs out. In an emergency, I *could* go to the chambers and try to get a 'present majority' vote on continuing business *without* the absent members, but that can't happen because the *entire* parliament is absent."

"So, effectively, you're Chancellor for life unless they decide to voluntarily come back from a fully paid, practically limitless vacation period."

"Pretty much."

"What happens if they all kick the bucket?"

"There's always going to be Old Martin," the Chancellor observed.

"Old Martin?"

"The oldest known member of parliament, first elected right at the very founding of the Federation. He was cursed by an indignant bloat-hag when he was a young man and has been doomed to sit in every session from then until she got back from her Aunt Tiffany's house over the weekend. Unfortunately, she died after choking on a three-bean salad, which meant that she never *did* return. So, Martin's been doomed to remain elected to parliament for all eternity. Even when it's been dissolved, Martin always just happens to be in the right place to miraculously survive. At least, that's the official story. Some say he's just a stuffed dummy rigged with wires to appear alive. Personally, I suspect that he's one of the immortal lizard men of

Krazelon dressed in an elaborate costume to bolster their voting power. He certainly does tend to vote in their favor a lot of the time."

Alexander stared at the Chancellor in bewilderment.

"Why the hell did you ever take this job?" he asked.

Bulbeeyoog let out a long sigh.

"My school counselor recommended it. He said it would have good *job security*, of all things."

A chime on the Chancellor's desk took the ensuing silence as an opportune moment to sound off. Bulbeeyoog picked up a laminated paper display off of the coffee table and poked it a few times.

"Ah, nuts. It looks like I'm going to have to run off to an appointment soon."

Bulbeeyoog hoisted himself upright, his attention focused on the display.

"Thank you for the chat, Alexander. It's nice to finally find someone even vaguely sympathetic to my predicament."

"No problem," Alexander replied. "I'm just happy to spend a few hours *not* being dragged off by strangers to who-knows-where."

"I know this wasn't the career you were looking for, Alexander, but I hope you'll stay on for a little while at least. I sure would appreciate the company every now and then."

"Hey, it's not exactly what I would usually think of as work, but if you're happy with the arrangement, I'm perfectly fine going along with it."

"I'm glad to hear that! I look forward to having more conversation, but for now, someone will be up in a minute to help guide you to your quarters. I wish I could say when we'll be able to meet again, but my schedule is a government secret."

"Well, it's not like I have much else on my plate. I guess I'll be around any time you need me."

"Sounds good, Alexander. Take care."

The Chancellor exited the office through a side door next to his desk, leaving Alexander sitting by himself on the massive couch. After a nicely timed pause, the front door opened to reveal the familiar aide who had greeted him in the audience chamber after his interview.

"Ahh... Mon-sigg-noar Ahl-ecks-aan-dur," the aide's forehead mouth exclaimed in a thick accent. "How fort-uit-ous is the comp-any of in your ple-asure."

"Uh, right," Alexander said dubiously. "Your name was Gleebo, wasn't it?"

"Gleeboh," the aide enunciated. "Glee-boh. But to such ser-vings of use in the matt-er is of none!"

Alexander narrowed his eyes a little, recalling the abrupt trans-formation in demeanor he'd caught a glimpse of before.

"Is this something you're doing on purpose?" he asked.

"Only the pur-pose-ment in do-ing to me is in ser-vic-ing of such in those to which such need is app-arrant-ing!" Gleeboh replied. "But such as the tim-ing and req-uire-ment-ings of in this space is to con-cur, re-quest-ment in most hum-ble terms to plee-as to move in as my follow-ment to the your of room."

To Smig's eyes, Gleeboh seemed to go out of his way to appear as condescending as possible as he tucked one arm behind his back and swept the other up to gesture at the door. The aide's upper mouth was frozen in a stock grin, while his lower held a wry smile. The more Smig interacted with Gleeboh, the more he was sure that the alien was deliberately being a dick. He had half a mind to be a dick right back, but despite having rested on a couch for a while, he felt exhausted and, more importantly, famished. Not the best time to pick fights with the help.

After stepping down from the couch, Alexander followed as the aide led him down a series of twisting corridors deeper into the gargantuan cruiser. They passed several security checkpoints, and Alexander was a little surprised at first that all of the security officers now seemed to immediately recognize him by sight, but he certainly had no complaints about getting waved right past some of the lines that were queued up between entry points. Eventually, the aide stopped and unlocked a sliding door, ushering Smig into a luxurious little apartment suite.

"The your of room, Mon-sigg-noar!" the aide said with a little presentational flourish. "If the your to be of any-thing is in of need-ing, give to mind of keep-ing the name is Gleeboh."

"Yeah, thanks. I'll remember that," Alexander replied, hoping desperately that there were other aides available if he genuinely needed help with anything.

Gleeboh made a little bow and took his leave, though he retained just the tiniest hint of a snarky, holier-than-thou smirk on his face as he did so.

"Don't blow a fuse trying," the aide muttered in a distinctly gruff tone.

Alexander spun around, but the door was already shut.

"You son of a bitch, I knew it!" he exclaimed.

Alexander had half a mind to go out and confront him, but right then, his stomach gurgled and reminded him it was entitled to compensation for what ended up in it... yesterday? He looked around for something like a clock or calendar, but there wasn't anything around that seemed remotely like either.

"Ah, forget it," he sighed.

Smig did his best to shrug the alien's attitude off and went to take a look around his new quarters. In terms of size, it wasn't much bigger than his old apartment on earth, but it was *definitely* fancier. A small kitchen-like area lined the wall on his right, while the left and center were open to hold a lounge-like circular sofa with an excellent view of space. Wandering a little closer, Alexander noticed that someone had gone around with a label maker and stuck little labels here and there. He bent down to read one attached to the wall.

"Rhomb-ohedron," it read, hyphen and all. "For the retrieve-ment of such your as items per-sonal."

"Ah," Alexander said out loud. "Let's see. I think Whoople said I just had to ask. Uh... could I have my backpack?"

"One moment," the rhombohedron buzzed mathematically. "Loading results... We have 1x portable strap-sack under the name Alexander Smig, with an assortment of various small items contained within. Also associated with this item is a separate ceramic vessel with extreme schlumbergera infestation. Do you wish to retrieve these items?"

"Yes?" Alexander said, not entirely sure what the second thing was.

"Beginning retrieval."

Half a blink and a comical pop later, and Alexander's bag and Christmas cactus popped back into existence, none the worse for wear.

"Holy shit!" Alexander remarked, briefly checking his things over. "Okay, that's pretty cool."

"Now listing contents to ensure safe receipt of all stowed materials," the rhombohedron declared. "One petrochemical enclosure containing genital-specific garments."

"Excuse me?" Alexander said.

"One pressurized capsule containing a white, goopy substance. Pictorial evidence suggests a type of facial lubricant."

"... My shaving cream?"

"Several highly ineffective prophylactics woven from organic textiles. The Federal Advisory Board for Containing Orgasms and Circumspect Kleptocracy recommends appropriately sized condoms manufactured from a nonporous material."

"Are you talking about my socks?" Alexander asked. "What the hell is-"

"Vanity sizing is available for those with low self-esteem."

"Now wait one fucking second-"

"One USB-*micro* charging cable," the rhombohedron continued unabated.

"Okay. You've got to be screwing with me now. You can't recognize a sock, but you know what a USB cable is? And I'm pretty sure you emphasized *micro* on purpose!"

"Sensors indicate biological flags suggesting a state of heightened aggression and/or arousal. F.A.B.C.O.C.K guidelines greatly discourage any actions which may result in bio-hazardous materials being released into the rhombohedron stowage system. Please resolve these concerns in an appropriate manner/receptacle before continuing with itemization."

The rhombohedron beeped and darkened a little as if some kind of interior light had been turned off. Smig stared dumbfounded at it for a minute, unsure how he should feel about the apparent suggestion that he might violate a cubby. Eventually, he decided to just

let it go. Alexander set his bag and cactus down on the little island/
breakfast bar in the kitchen, muttering to himself.

"What the hell have I gotten myself into," he said, taking a moment to look the cactus over and make sure it hadn't been bruised or
anything. "Well, at least you don't seem any worse for wear."

Alexander poked a finger down into the soil. It was still damp
about an inch down, perfect for a cactus like this and just as he'd left
it. Glancing over the contents of his bag confirmed that everything
seemed to be in order, so he turned to the task of seeing what was
around to eat.

The dimensions of the kitchen were a little odd, but the layout
and appliances didn't seem particularly out of whack. He decided
to start by opening the fridge and was greeted by the sight of
about six or seven fake, potted plants stacked on the shelves, all
of which were loudly humming ominously. A particularly large
█████████████ {FLOWERING SHRUB} on the bottom
rack seemed to hum even louder than the others as if the fresh
ingress of air and light was particularly hateful to it.

Alexander stood transfixed for a little while, staring with more
than a little trepidation at the menacing contents of the fridge,
before he noticed a little placard standing off to one side which read:

'A little taste of home: Earth cuisine by Zarap Teleyqua, Head Legumier
of the Federal Universal Cruiser Kerflidivitz.'

Alexander slowly closed the refrigerator and took a step back.
He was now keenly aware that the low, rumbling hum he had assumed to be coming from the appliance was instead a product of its
contents.

"I hope there's something I can eat around here," he said quietly,
hoping to dispel this turn of events from his mind.

Mercifully, he managed to find some prepackaged '*import Earth
food*' in a cupboard that he could more-or-less identify. Deciding to
eschew the tins of pâté that were printed in a Cyrillic alphabet, he
pulled out a box of macaroni and cheese, or '*Coquilles et fromage*' as it
was labeled in French. After fooling around for some time working
out how to boil a totally spherical pot of water over what was ba-

sically an open-flame Bunsen burner, Alexander managed to make himself a half-decent meal.

After eating, he relaxed for a while. It was somewhat disorienting to have no outside reference for the passage of time, but he distracted himself for a bit by exploring the features of his room. The bathroom seemed to operate more or less as it should (which was a relief), and the bed in the bedroom was quite large and exceedingly comfy. Despite the oddities in the kitchen, it was obvious that someone had taken greater than usual efforts to make the space feel more Earth-like. He was just toying around with a large panel of glass on the wall by the sofa he figured was supposed to work like some kind of television when something in his bag started buzzing.

Alexander approached it somewhat warily until he realized it was his cell phone going off. Hastily pulling it out, he saw his old boss Jerry was calling.

"Hello?" he asked.

"Alex?" Jerry replied. "Is that you? This is Jerry."

"Hey, Jerry. I'm kinda surprised we've got a connection right now."

"You're telling me! I'm in Nome, Alaska and it's a God damn miracle we got here. You ever see that movie Balto where they run the sled dogs halfway across Alaska to deliver medicine?"

"Maybe once as a kid." Smig said.

"Well, we just did that but with a train of pack mules. Got stranded on a mountain for almost 2 hours while a pissed-off moose blocked our path and afterwards nearly slid into ravines I don't know how many times. The Iditarod is no place for a mule, much less ten of them!"

"Holy shit. I take it you weren't able to talk Ellie out of her plans then?"

"No! And as a matter of fact, she still wants to hike up to Utqa-Utkee... what used to be Barrow Alaska. Over 500 miles away as the crow flies with zero road access. The craziest thing is we somehow seem to be skirting around all the shit going down everywhere else on Earth so far. How are you doing? I heard you got into a new job?"

"Uh, yeah. You could say that."

"Good deal. I had some wacko call asking weird questions about you, so I hoped you were doing all right."

"Yeah, things have been... weird. But I think I'm doing okay for now."

"That's good to hear. Man, it's hard to believe just a few weeks ago we were..."

Jerry trailed off. Smig heard him yelling away from the phone.

"Ellie! What the hell are those?" he shouted distantly.

Alexander couldn't hear the reply, but Jerry didn't seem too happy with whatever it was.

"They're what?" he cried. "Where the hell did you get those? ... No! ... No, you're not getting me to ride one of those!"

Jerry's voice came back to the phone.

"I gotta go, Alex. Ellie just showed up with a team of fucking Tibetan Yaks pulling a sled. If you don't hear from me for a long while, I've either frozen to death or been eaten by polar bears."

"Okay, Jerry. Take care."

"You too."

The phone blipped out, leaving Alexander with the conclusion that he could be in a much worse situation, even considering the outlandish comedy of errors that had deposited him here. Sinking into the couch, he reflected on the last few days and where he was now. It wasn't all bad, but he couldn't help pinching himself because it sure was one hell of a weird dream.

Chapter 13
The Close Encounter

Alexander awoke to the sound of a chime tinkling from the front door. He got up with a start, taking a moment to recognize the unfamiliar surroundings of his apartment on the Federal Cruiser.

"Hello?" a deep, feminine voice said over an intercom. "Alexander Smig?"

"Oh uh, hello?" Alexander replied as he turned around to face the door. "Can you hear me?"

"I can hear you, Alexander. I hope I'm not disturbing you."

"No, uh. Just a second."

Alexander hefted himself up and stumbled over to the door. There still wasn't any recognizable time-keeping devices anywhere, so he could only guess how long he'd been napping. Approaching the door, he stared in vain for a knob or a peephole. As far as he could tell, there wasn't even a button or panel to poke at or anything. Briefly, he tried to decipher some of Gleeboh's labels stuck around the frame, the vast majority of which were entirely unhelpful.

"Sorry!" he said. "I'm having some trouble figuring out how to open this thing."

"You should be able to pass a hand or something near the door frame," The lady suggested. "But you have to picture an open door in your mind at the same time. Keeps it from opening accidentally."

Alexander gave the door a perplexed look and waved his hands around. To his surprise, it finally slid open the moment he focused on a mental image of an open door. This revealed an alien that was a little more unusual than most Smig had seen up to this point. At first glance, her general appearance was very snake-like. She sported two arms in a little torso-like section at the base of her long neck, but beyond that was just a long coil, ending in a tail that seemed to have its own hand with two claws. Given the particulars of her proportions, she wasn't wearing much for clothing save for a flowing length of material that served as a top.

"Hello, Alexander," she said. "I hope you don't mind me stopping by. It's not very often that we get someone new on board who isn't here for business or politics. I wanted to introduce myself. My name is Martheena."

"Oh, well uh... you already seem to know who I am. Would you, um, want to come in for a minute?"

"I would love to!"

Alexander wasn't entirely sure why he'd offered the invitation, but Martheena seemed to have a certain poise that activated his manners, like whenever he had talked with his 98 year-old neighbor Mrs. Svenslaand. He moved aside to let Martheena slither her way past. It was a good thing he didn't have any phobias related to big snakes since she was comfortably four or five times as long as he was tall. Despite her large size, she kept herself drawn up roughly equal with him to make for easy eye contact. Gliding through the room, she coiled up by the sofa as Alexander took a seat across from her.

"I understand you're fairly new to the Federation, Alexander," Martheena prompted as they got comfortable.

"Yeah," he said, sighing a little. "It's been... an *interesting* experience so far."

"Bulby's told me a little bit about the adventures you've had."

"Bulby?" Alexander asked.

"My husband, Bulbeeyoog," Martheena replied.

"Oh! I'm sorry. He never mentioned he was married."

"Oh no, he wouldn't, of course," Martheena assured him. "It's just a political marriage, after all. We're on good terms with each other, but as marriages go, it's nothing to write home about."

"I see," Alexander replied. "Uh, sorry if this comes across as a strange question, but is it... okay for him to hire a concubine if he's married?"

Martheena gave a little, dismissive laugh.

"It's certainly fine with me. Concubines are respected professionals in the Federation, and no self-respecting politician hires anybody if they thought it would cause a row. Maybe Lunatic Lorenzo, but even he's pretty level-headed about *that* sort of thing. Even if that weren't the case, I know the real reason why he hired you, Alexander. I *do* think it's a little silly that paperwork of all things seems to get under his skin so much, but everybody's got their own little foibles."

Here she leaned forward and whispered conspiratorially.

"Speaking of which, did he ask you to braid his hair?"

"Well, uh... yeah, he did."

Martheena drew back and laughed in earnest.

"I knew he would!" she replied merrily. "He always asks me, but I can hardly do anything dexterous with these clumsy claws."

She held up her hands, which sported only two clawed fingers each, with no opposable thumb.

"Truthfully, I'm glad we've finally got someone around who can help scratch odd little itches like that. You'd be amazed how much little actions can add up to improve your quality of life."

"I guess so," Smig said. "I still kinda find it hard to believe that until I stumbled into this that he couldn't find someone who was willing to just listen to him complain for a few hours."

"Oh, there's always some obsequious toady willing to do whatever in exchange for attention, but Bulby's always had a real distaste for fawning sycophants. Whatever brought him on to you, I'm sure he feels that you understand his frustration and sympathize with it. That is a fine quality indeed."

"Coming from a job in heavy labor, it still just feels strange to get paid for *'raising someone's spirits.'*"

"Darling, that's what concubines are *for*," she replied. "And you're the only one he's had since I've been with him. Both of us have wanted to introduce an extra element around here to keep things from being so *boring*, but it took such a long time to get arrangements worked out. Like I mentioned earlier, everyone else who comes on board is here for business, politics, or security and nothing else. Friend and Family visits are strictly limited to special occasions, and even then, they're tricky to arrange. I genuinely can't stress enough how nice it is to have someone you can just talk to without having to worry about offending their stockholders or constituents. Just... vent some cepilation that's been pent up in the narbles for a while, if you'll excuse the expression."

Alexander didn't know what that meant, but he nodded politely anyway. Martheena smiled and idly traced a claw across her coils.

"Of course, being a simple figurehead, my own schedule is far less complicated than my husband's. Yet still, even I don't have the luxury of frequent casual interactions. It legitimately take a dedicated hire under your own roof to satisfy the security concerns enough to be able to do that. Which is why I'm very glad you're here now. Of course, I'm glad that Bulby is happy, but I do have a few of my own '*odd little itches*' that wouldn't mind being scratched."

Smig almost second-guessed himself over the flagrantly suggestive tone Martheena had just used, but the near-predatory look she now flashed at him seemed to confirm she had less-than-saintly intentions.

"Ah," He replied. "How would your husband feel about that?"

"Oh, don't worry. Bulby and I have an understanding. He has priority for your attention, naturally, but when he's busy with other things, he doesn't mind if I ask you for favors. Of course, I would never demand anything that you would consider unreasonable."

"I suppose that sounds all right, but something tells me you're thinking of something other than having me try to braid hair."

"Well, of course," she said, gesturing to indicate her complete lack of the stuff. "But, you see, Alexander, one of the reasons that Bulby wasn't terribly interested in your '*intimate abilities*' was the fact that part of his job as Chancellor involves an *exhausting* amount of '*personal negotiations*' with political friends, foes, and whatever in between. It's a very demanding aspect of his day-to-day life, to the point where it's simply not feasible for him to have any fun with me, save for the rare special occasion."

"Ah,"

"I don't blame him, of course. His job is a real pain in the ass in more ways than one. But given the situation, I can assure you that Bulby has no objection to me seeking other companionship as long as I'm open about it. Even with his blessing, there's so much concern over '*unsavory outside influences*' and whatnot from the muckrakers in the system that I still hardly get a chance. *However*, seeing as you're employed specifically for intimate purposes, nobody would really mind if you paid *me* a visit every now and again... What do you think, Alexander?"

"Well," he said thoughtfully. "You did hear how I ended up as a concubine, right? I'm not exactly the most um, experienced guy out there."

"I'm not exactly the pickiest girl," Martheena laughed. "Of course, if you'd rather not, I won't bother you about it."

Here she leaned in close.

"It's just that I've spent so many long nights with no other option but to manually file QSG forms by myself if you know what I mean. I'd really, *really* enjoy the attention."

Martheena maintained a respectful distance between them, but there was nothing to hide the brief quiver of excitement that briefly tensed down the length of her entire body. Alexander wasn't exactly sure how he felt about getting cozy with a giant snake alien, but it seemed she could barely contain her eagerness. It probably wouldn't be as bad as riding a yak across some 500-odd miles of arctic tundra, he thought to himself.

"Well," he said. "So long as you're sure I'm not going to get in trouble with anyone over this."

"Believe me, as long as I'm not keeping you from Bulby's little hair braiding sessions, it's fine."

"Then I guess I'm okay with trying things out."

"Yay!" Martheena shook her hands excitedly (including the one on the tip of her tail) before leaning forward again with a grin. "I'm so excited, Alexander. Now, I don't want to seem too desperate, but could I convince you to put some hours in?"

"You mean like, right now?"

Martheena had already started sliding along the ring of the couch towards him with a cocky look in her eyes. She stopped just close enough that he could notice the warmth that seemed to radiate from her skin.

"It's been such a long time since I could be with someone," she said. "Can I *indulge*? I promise I can make it worth your while."

"Sounds like it would be almost criminal to stop you at this point," Alexander replied. "Just keep in mind I'm still new to, um... interspecies interactions."

Martheena laughed and put her hands on his shoulders.

"Nothing like some on-the-job instruction," she whispered in his ear. "I think you'll pick things up pretty quickly."

In one smooth motion, Martheena slid her hands from Alexander's shoulders up to cup his head and draw him into a kiss. Given the discrepancy in size, Alexander's mouth was almost fully enveloped in her voluptuous lips. Martheena pressed into Alexander, gently bending him backwards to both prolong the kiss and bring herself right up against him. She ran her hands up through his hair and back down across his chest. Buried in her face, Alexander felt her entire warm body vibrate softly as she moaned. Caught up in the action, he ran his own hands along her sides, slipping up underneath the light cloth veil she wore for a top. Martheena broke off the kiss with a light pop.

"Hah, I'd like to take your clothes off, Alexander," she said, stroking him. "But I'm afraid I just don't have that kind of finesse."

She held up one of her two-clawed hands to demonstrate the problem.

"That's all right," Alexander said. "Here..."

Martheena pulled back just enough to let him take off his shirt and pants while she slipped off what little of her own clothing there was. Honestly, she didn't have much to cover up. Despite the curvy nature of her torso, she had no breasts, and further down, there was only a fold in her skin to suggest where her privates hid themselves.

There may not have been that much to look at (From an Earthling perspective), but Martheena made up for that with how she used it. No sooner had Alexander disrobed than she dived on him again for another deep kiss. Now she ran her hands down his back and explored the length and breadth of his body. Alexander did his best not to get knocked over by her barely restrained enthusiasm. He was caught by surprise when she suddenly gripped him firmly in her arms and hoisted him off of the couch and into the middle of her coils. Martheena laid him down on his back and positioned the base of her torso between his legs, lowering herself into a tight embrace on top of him as she breathed, moaned, and continued her enveloping kiss.

"Mnn, you're pretty eager, aren't you?" Alexander managed to murmur out one side of his mouth.

"Oh!" Martheena gasped slightly. "You have no idea, Alexander. Now just relax and let me loosen up a little."

Once again, those luscious lips took claim over his. Martheena's whole body was twisting now, slowly writhing pleasurably on every side of him. Alexander ran his hands across her and noticed that her smooth skin had suddenly started to feel slick. He'd almost forgotten about the depuration tablet that Grand Master Whoople had given him but now assumed that it must be the source of this vaguely slippery feeling. The more Martheena moved, the more Alexander felt like he was being coated in something. It wasn't oily or unpleasant in any way. In fact, here and now, it seemed to have a kind of calming effect on his muscles and joints.

"How do you feel, Alexander?" Martheena broke off just long enough to ask.

"Very nice," Alexander replied almost dreamily. "Very relaxing, whatever's in those tablet things."

"Depuration tablets?" she asked.

"Yeah, those."

"Well," Martheena giggled. "They might be helping a bit, but I've got my own natural method of keeping you relaxed, lubricated, and *pliable*."

"Pliab-"

Alexander's confusion was cut off by the resumption of her smooching assault. The odd word stuck in his mind despite the calming effect of the oils Martheena's body was producing. Whatever it was, it was quick and tremendously potent. He could feel the years of knots untangling themselves in his back and shoulders. Any strain or tiredness in his limbs was being snuffed out for a surprisingly nice numb sensation, distinctly different from the numbing that had happened after the slyger incident. A dreamy euphoria descended on Smig, not quite a haze in his mind, but more like a blanket order for everything to just chill out and not worry.

Given this dream-like, relaxed state that was taking over his head, it took a few moments for it to sink in that something wasn't quite right. Alexander couldn't quite pick out what it was until he shifted enough in Martheena's embrace to notice that his one arm was doubled back at an impossible angle. He didn't experience any pain or feel like he had lost control of anything. His arm and everything else had become as soft and malleable as rubber. Smig's mind belatedly registered this turn of events before he noticed another sensation. Between himself and the gargantuan alien snake, something much more like an earth-sized snake was slithering up between his legs.

Martheena had been rubbing her fold against his upper thighs up to this point, and now a tentacle-like pseudo-■■■■■ *{LANCELOT}* had emerged and wormed its way between their tightly embracing bodies. It squirmed next to his own ■■■■■ *{TOY SOLDIER}* and clearly surpassed it, coming all the way up to his belly button. Again, Martheena released his lips with a light pop and drew herself up a little. Alexander could move but felt so wobbly that he wasn't sure he could even lift up his head without it flopping over. Martheena's coils wriggled underneath his body, repositioning him.

"Yes," Martheena cooed. "Nice and flexible, so this shouldn't hurt at all. In fact, this should feel *very* nice for both of us."

Martheena leaned down again, gripping her pseudo-██████ {PITCHFORK} and aiming it at his exposed ████ {TUCKUS}. Part of him wanted to panic, but he wasn't sure he could even speak coherently anymore with how rubbery he had become. Alexander had one last indignant thought as she bore down on him.

'*I guess I got myself into this, but why is it all* ███████ *{SAU-SAGES} for me out here in space?*'

Martheena pressed her member into Alexander's ███████ {WORMHOLE}. It felt like his entire body was being stretched and expanded around her █████ {THIRD LEG} as she slowly fed it in inch by inch. She heaved a sigh as her base finally pressed up against his rump. Gently she dropped herself onto his bulging stomach for another embrace. Both her arms and coils ran over him as she invaded his lips yet again, drawing in a forceful intake of breath.

Alexander could barely move or think, but something had now supplanted the disjointed concern that had been there before. Now all he could focus on was how amazing this felt. He wasn't sure if there was something in whatever he was covered in that altered his state of mind, but he seemed sensitive to every touch and movement that Martheena made both inside and out, and she was laying them on thick. The snake-like writhing of her coils gave him a near full-body massage while her hands kept him close and tight to her chest.

Now she arched her back and started to drive herself in and out of his ███ {CAVERNS}. Martheena started slowly but clearly was struggling to contain herself. Waves of warmth and pleasure rocked Alexander from the bottom up as she started ███████ {CHECK-ING THE OIL} in earnest. The sensation reminded him of Whoople's incredible blowjob, but this time from the inside out, as his murky mind put it. Soon she was rolling back and forth so vigorously that her base began to slap noisily against his █████ {BREAD BASKET}. Breaking off her stranglehold on his lips, she wrapped her arms around his head and shoulders, grunting and moaning loudly. All Alexander could manage was try to keep his arms and legs wrapped around her torso, to keep them from flapping or bouncing around in their rubbery state as she ██████ {HID THE BISHOP} hard.

Martheena's moans turned into rising cries of pleasure each time she rapidly ██████ {PARALLEL PARKED} into him. With little warning, she suddenly squeezed him tight and drove home as deep into his ███ {GORGE} as she could. Alexander felt his entire body twist awkwardly in her tight embrace as she tensed all of her muscles in ecstasy. Her whole body twitched violently and jerked as she rocked through an ██████ {OVATION}.

However, something strange was going on, for now, it felt like the alien's ████ {CYCLOPEAN SERPENT} was getting thicker. Martheena tensed again, and a bulging mass muscled its way up into his ████████ {WHOOPTY-DOO}. Despite the concerning nature of this progressing event, the intense sensation it brought on quickly sent Alexander over the edge. He moaned unconsciously as his ███ {MILKSHAKE} shot up across his bulging stomach and onto his chest. This ecstasy distracted him from what felt like a baseball winding up the █████ {CANDY DISPENSER} he was impaled upon. Now past the threshold, Smig's internal passages stretched with ease and gave no resistance as the lump traveled to the end of her pseudo-█████ {PUMPERNICKEL}. As it reached her tip, Martheena jerked again and cried out as she released it into his gut. She spasmed, involuntarily ███████ {TESTING THE SUSPEN-SION} a few more times before she finally collapsed, panting on top of him.

"Oh, Alexander," she whispered, almost out of breath. "That was amazing! You don't know how long I've been waiting for this."

"Mmmlurrgeburr..." was all he managed to mumble.

"Sorry," Martheena giggled. "I forget the relaxant makes it hard to talk sometimes."

She cupped his head with her hands and gave him a more modest kiss. Alexander was too wracked with bliss to do much.

"It's never the same when you're just filing forms by yourself," Martheena said, with a definite innuendo that time. "Always so much nicer when you have someone else to share the load. Ever since I heard that Bulby was hiring a concubine, I've been looking forward to this. I think I've saved up at least five more eggs."

Alexander's eyes flicked open wide as Martheena's lips got adventurous and explored his cheeks. She seemed to be working herself up again, breathing deeply as she embraced and molded his entire body. Once again, she slowly drew her pseudo-████ {BREADSTICK} out, only to slide it home again. Alexander was now very concerned over whether he could handle five more rounds of this, but the foggy haze of bliss had already started enveloping his mind once again, and his thoughts were quickly lost as she continued to ████ {GO SPELUNKING}.

Somewhere amidst the ceaseless, pounding pleasure, Alexander had lost track of time. Overwhelmed by pleasure and Martheena's psychoactive oils, he could do little else but lay there while Martheena continuously ███████ ███████ {INITIATED A JOINT SESSION OF CONGRESS}, pausing only occasionally to pump another baseball-sized egg into him. His stomach was now distended almost beyond the point of most pregnant women, yet still, the alien continued her ███████ {INTERIOR DECORATING}.

No longer able to comfortably lie on top of him, she had at some point flipped him over and draped him over her tail. She was bent over him now, ███████ {HARPOONING} his elevated ████ {WHALE} while her hands massaged his overextended belly. Moaning, she started her quickening crescendo of staccato cries to signal another oncoming █████ {CHATTANOOGA CHOO-CHOO}. Driving her ███ {SECRET AGENT} deep, she practically screamed as the egg pressed past his ████████ {SALLY PORT} and wound up his insides. Forced out of her █████ {HAMMER DRILL}, it shoved the others out of its way and further extended Alexander's taxed form. Again, Martheena collapsed with a long, gratifying sigh.

"That's seven," she breathed with a little smile. "And I think I might have just one more left in me."

Alexander groaned inside his head. He had lost track of how many times he'd ███ {SET OFF FIREWORKS} himself, but it had to have been a lot.

"It's not often that I've had eight eggs saved up," Martheena continued through her kisses. "I want you to have them all, Alexander. I want to-"

She was interrupted by the chime at the front door. Chancellor Bulbeeyoog's voice came on the intercom.

"Alexander? Are you in there?" he asked.

Martheena jumped and fully withdrew herself from Alexander's ██████ {RABBIT WARREN} with one sloppy pop. She quickly threw her coils over Alexander, literally covering him up.

"Uh... no!" Martheena answered shakily. "I'm here, though, Bulby."

Alexander burbled incoherently. He was in no position mentally or physically to do much, but he got the impression that Martheena was hastily wrapping herself back up in her clothes. A light swooshing noise and some vibrations indicated that the towering chancellor had entered the room.

"Martheena?" Bulbeeyoog asked. "Where's Alexander?"

"Your new concubine, Mr. Smig?" Martheena replied. "Why we were having a nice conversation, but he stepped out for a moment. He asked where the decarbonizer was, and I gave him some directions."

Even underneath the coils, Alexander could hear the Chancellor's exasperated sigh.

"Earthlings don't need to decarbonize, Martheena. Have you been causing trouble?"

"Certainly not!" she replied defensively.

"Your skin is soaking with oils, and... are those his clothes on the floor there?"

"Bulby, listen. You've got the wrong idea."

"Uncoil yourself, Martheena."

"You don't understand. We were just talking. He just stepped out for a minute."

"Then uncoil yourself."

"No!"

"Martheena Gergohnda Mistiqwa Simpson!" Bulbeeyoog said sternly. "You will uncoil yourself, or you will be grounded for an entire yelaageroo!"

"Don't you use my full name at me, Francine Abner Bulbeeyoog! You're not my father!"

"I can get your father! Want me to go release him from the dungeon?"

"You wouldn't dare!"

"Try me!"

There was a moment of tense silence, presumably Bulbeeyoog and his wife were staring each other down. Martheena finally gave a frustrated grunt and moved her tail to reveal a very full and disheveled Alexander sprawled on the floor.

"Oh, for the love of Globbo!" the Chancellor slapped his forehead. "Martheena! I told you *multiple times* not to lay eggs in him!"

"They're not fertilized!" Martheena whined. "A couple duds aren't going to hurt him."

"Look at how big he is!" Bulbeeyoog shouted in exasperation. "How many did you lay in him?"

"Seven," she replied haughtily. "I almost got to eight."

"I told you, humans don't have any ability to handle them on their own. If he derubberizes before they're removed, he'll pop like a whiz-bang. I'm calling for a doctor. *You* are going to your room."

The chancellor came into Alexander's view. He bent down, ignoring Martheena's protestations.

"Can you hear me, Alexander?" he asked.

"Gighphbh gegg... l'egg," Alexander slurred.

"I see," the Chancellor said. "Hang on. Help is coming."

Smig's mind had been slipping for some time, and it decided that now was the perfect time to check out.

Chapter 14
The Morning After

Alexander awoke. Once again, he felt groggy and dead-limbed, but at least this time around, he was buried in an exceptionally comfortable bed. He had been transported to a clean, medical-looking room filled with life support equipment and tacky paintings, one of which appeared to be some kind of arthropod trying desperately not to fall off of a crystalline structure while encouraging the reader to 'hang in there.'

Gingerly, he shifted a little to see if he was still rubbery. To his relief, his hand was no longer capable of bending itself around and grabbing his own forearm.

'Guh,' he thought to himself. 'I guess that's something."

Hesitantly, he lifted his head to peer over the blankets. To Alexander's great relief, his stomach was no longer a gargantuan, distended balloon. With a sigh, he let his head fall back into the pillows.

A vague, woozy thought meandered into his mind, and wondered if he'd simply had one hell of a strange dream or possibly a drug trip. Alexander didn't think *any* kind of drug could make him hallucinate things as weird as what he could remember, but he was also having a hard time believing that he'd been basically turned into a Stretchable McHarmstrung toy. Idly, he wondered if there were any visible stretch marks on his person.

"No, you won't have any," a voice answered. "We managed to remove the '*foreign objects*' and get you back to normal proportions before the rubberization effect wore off."

Alexander frowned and tipped his head up to see where the voice had come from. A tall individual floated into the room on some kind of strange, mechanical platform. Said alien's appearance was something approximating a skinny, bald black bear with a cuttlefish head and many-jointed arms. On his forehead, there appeared to be a black, temporary tattoo of a rhombohedron that was already starting to peel off in spots.

"How'd you know what I was thinking?" Alexander asked with a gummy mouth.

"Quite simple, actually," the alien replied. "That was the mind reader we keep on to monitor your sleep. Somewhat concerning to me how much your unconscious mind seemed to fixate on inexplicable scenarios involving wetting the bed. However, I must admit, my study of Earthling medical science has been primarily focused on the physiological rather than the psychological, so it could be perfectly normal."

He took a moment to flip a few switches on a nearby console before turning around to stare at some readout charts by the bedside.

"Now then, Mr. Smig. My name is Doctor Yew. As you can see by my identifying tattoo, I am a Federally conditioned physician, which means I am specially trained to provide care for the highest ranking political members in the F.O.E. and would never sell confidential information to any disreputable tabloids. It's up to them if they want to misrepresent your public dream record as evidence of secret, lurid fetishes. In any case, I am happy to say that although you may expect some amount of discomfort for a few hours, you have not suffered any long-term effects and should make a complete recovery."

"Well... that's good," Alexander replied with some mixed emotions.

"Indeed. How are you feeling right now?"

"Uh... You know, I think I'm okay. I feel groggy, but not bad."

"Excellent! Now, before I take my leave, I have been asked to relay the Chancellor's apologies for the incident that occurred last quardecilaagaroo and assurances that his wife will not be allowed unsupervised visitations without your express permission from this point on."

"Okay. Thanks, Doc."

"Not at all! When you are ready to leave, there will be an aide at the desk outside your room to help guide you wherever you may wish to go. Take it easy for a while, and rest assured any ugly rumors you may hear about yourself after this were clumsily derived from publicly accessible data and not from a lucrative breach in confidentiality."

With that, Doctor Yew skedoodled out of the room on his floating machine. Alexander blinked for a moment, gathering his wits. He wasn't sure if he was getting used to the crazy people in the Federation or if his judgment was clouded from waking up a hot mess every morning for the last few days. Eventually, he decided he'd rather not think about that and pulled the blankets away. Hoisting himself up, he came to a sudden stop.

"Oh..." he said quietly.

Alexander had never taken anything up the ████ {KRAMPUS} like that before, and the aftermath sensations were certainly something to get used to. He rapidly discovered he was sore in places he didn't even know he had. Nothing that stopped him from getting up and moving around, but his legs were definitely a little wobbly at first. It also didn't help that the hospital gown he was wearing freely admitted a draft, which seemed intent on boldly going where no draft had gone before. Gritting his teeth, he staggered to the door and pulled it open.

"Ah, Mon-sigg-noar Ahl-ecks-aan-dur!" cried a familiar voice. "How is for to feel in the way of your, this morn-ing fine?"

Alexander gave Gleeboh a long, hard squint. He toyed with the idea of trying to comprehend the alien's question but quickly decided he just wasn't in a mood to try and deal with him.

"What an unexpected surprise," Alexander said flatly. "You don't happen to know if I have any clothes here?"

Gleeboh saw his squint and raised him a sneer.

"Afraid is Gleeboh the cloth-ing of Mon-sigg-noar is not of the way in being of as now."

"I'll take that as a no," Smig sighed. "Listen, I don't want to walk very far. Is there somewhere nearby where I can just sit for a while and maybe get some food?"

"Sir-tain-lee!" the aide exclaimed. "A place-ing for food the of order-ing. Plee-as to move in as my follow-ment."

Gleeboh swept past him and took up an exaggerated march down the hallway. Alexander half-limped, half-staggered after him. If he hadn't been so tired, stiff, and sore, he probably would have been a little more shy as the aide led him out of the medical wing. As it was, he simply kept the part down his back scrunched closed with one hand as they came up to something that looked like a cheap little airport terminal bistro. By the way Gleeboh turned and grinned at him, Alexander could only assume that the aide had intended this to be some kind of joke at his expense.

"The finest in nothing of best for you," Gleeboh declared with a wry smile.

Smig grunted and began to stagger up to a seat. As he passed Gleeboh, he clearly heard the alien murmur something.

"Don't let the stool go all the way up when you try to sit on it."

Something snapped in Alexander's head. He didn't stop to think, he simply turned and punched Gleeboh right in the squirmy little tentacle where his nose should be. The aide collapsed to the floor, and Smig flinched a little in surprise as only now did his self-control catch up to him. Before he could say anything, Gleeboh sat up.

"Whoo!" the alien exclaimed, without any trace of an accent. "It's about damn time you tipped."

"What?

"I was starting to think you were just stingy or something, but man! That was a good one!"

"You wanted me to punch you?" Alexander asked in confusion.

"Hey, now," Gleeboh remarked, standing up and dusting himself off. "I'm not greedy! Some verbal abuse or maybe a slap now and again is fine enough for me, but if you're throwing out punches, I'm not complaining."

"You take abuse as tips?"

"Of course! Why do you think I've been so rude? But anyway, don't let me keep you from breakfast. If you need anything else, just push a call button and ask for Gleeboh!"

Smig peered at the alien as he strode away. Finally, he shook his head and turned back towards the bistro. At this point, he just wanted to sit down and get something to eat. The whole place was empty, which suited him just fine. Smig took a seat at the front counter and picked up a menu. He was lazily perusing the grand total of three options available when a greasy-looking chef, sporting a mustache that looked like an old broom head, wandered out of the kitchen.

"What'll ya have today?" the Chef asked in an outrageously nasal voice.

"Uh, is there anything else on the menu besides eggs, bacon, and spam?"

"Wait a minute!" the Chef exclaimed. "Alexander, is that you?"

"Uh, yeah?" Alexander said uneasily, looking up from the menu.

"Hey! It's me, Ryan Schmidtke!"

The Chef ripped off his fake mustache, which *was* an old broom head, to reveal that he was, in fact, the professional kidnapper.

"Holy shit!" Alexander exclaimed. "You were eaten alive right before my eyes! What the hell are you doing here?"

"Well, thankfully, slygers don't have a true digestive system. I'll spare you the grimy details, but I managed to give Zloykot the slip and hail a passing taxi. From there, I dodged around a bit until I could pick up one of my cover jobs, which just happened to be the Chef of this fine little bistro."

"Isn't it a little ballsy to hide out on the Chancellor's ship?"

"This is the Chancellor's cruiser!?" Ryan asked with genuine surprise. "Cripes! Does he know that *you're* here?"

"Actually, yeah. Turns out things are cool."

"Seriously? That's a relief. Are you still pretending to be a concubine?"

"Well, uh... Wait, what do you mean pretending?"

"It was pretty obvious from the get-go that you don't have any actual experience. I mean, you didn't even recognize this bad boy when I whipped it out for the contract."

"Oh for fucks sake! Could you not wave that around? I was planning on eating breakfast."

"All right," Ryan chuckled, stashing away his dildo. "But anyways, you didn't really wind up with the job, did ya?"

"I kinda did."

"No way!" the alien exclaimed excitedly. "Are you really ███████ ███████ *{BURPING THE WORM IN THE MOLE HOLE}* with the Chancellor himself?"

"Not exactly," Alexander said. "Listen, we worked out a deal, but it's complicated and probably considered a state secret for all I know. Maybe we can talk about it later, but I had one hell of a night and, right now, I just want something to eat."

"No problemo, you rascal!" Ryan said with a cheeky wink. "Our special today is fresh eggs!"

Alexander winced.

"Do you have anything else?" he asked.

"Uh..." Ryan scratched his head and counted his fingers. "...Nope! Just eggs right now."

"Where did the eggs come from?" Alexander asked suspiciously.

"Local suppliers."

"On or off the ship?"

"Off the ship, of course. Where would I even get eggs onboard? Nobody keeps egg-laying space ducks on cruisers like this, just those majestic breeds they keep as pets."

"Okay, fine. I'll do some eggs."

"All right! One plate of eggs, coming right up!"

One plate of spotted purple eggs sunny-side-up later, Ryan took a seat next to Alexander.

"You know, Ryan," Alexander said between mouthfuls. "I hate to admit you were right, but the pâté actually does go pretty well with it,"

"I told you so," Ryan replied. "You gotta try it with waffles sometime."

"We'll see. Are you hanging around here for a while? It's kind of nice to have someone comparatively less insane to talk to."

"Yeah, I'll be here awhile. I'd rather wait and see if a contract comes along rather than try to pick up random cold cases for the time being."

"Can't imagine why."

Ryan chuckled a little and sighed. There was a bit of a pause, and Alexander turned to look around the bistro.

"Something wrong?" Ryan asked.

"Well, it's just that every meal I've had the last couple of days has ended with me being nabbed by goons of some type or another and dragged off for parts unknown."

"Relax, Alexander. We're not just on any old scram shuttle. We're on the Chancellor's personal cruiser! Just about the safest and most secure place in the entire multiverse. The likelihood of anything bad happening here is almost infinitesima-"

A gigantic, thuddering whump echoed from somewhere far away in the ship. The lights flickered as the entire cruiser suddenly shook and listed to one side. Everything in the bistro that wasn't nailed down started sliding across the walkway towards the great viewing windows. Dishes crashed loudly as they fell off of shelves, and both Ryan and Alexander found themselves smushed face first into the glass as tables, chairs, and various contents from the kitchen piled up around them. Peeling themselves off the window, they watched as a smaller, ragged spaceship maneuvered around the Chancellor's cruiser and lined up broadside with guns bristling out in every direction.

"What the hell is that!?" Alexander shouted.

"A gunship!" Ryan squeaked through the egg all over his face. "We're under attack!"

"Who the hell would be attacking?"

"I can only think of eight people who would be bold enough to assault the Chancellor in open space! Let's see... It's hard to make out the ship markings at this distance, but those are the wrong colors for Grungleda the Peeved. Uh... It wouldn't be Bulbeeyoog's mother-in-law Maude, since she's still trapped in the maze of insanity...

Maybe it's Jarva Argoh Lohpia of the Functionally Underestimated Committee of Kumquats, Eggplants, and Red Squash."

"ATTENTION!" a voice blared out over the ship-wide intercom. "THE CRUISER IS EXPERIENCING A MILD AFFRONT. ALL PASSENGERS ARE REQUESTED TO RETURN TO THEIR QUARTERS OR WAIT IN THE GREAT HALL. PLEASE DO NOT PANIC AND TAKE THIS TIME TO FILL OUT THE PRO-VIDED LIABILITY WAIVERS."

"I don't know where anything on this ship is!" Alexander said. "Can we hide in your kitchen?"

"Well, considering there's now broken glass all over everything in there, I'm going to vote for the main hall. It's not far from here."

"You know where to go?"

"Sure do! Come on!"

The two of them took off down the hall. Alexander followed Ryan as closely as he could while still trying to keep his hospital gown in place as the draft played an unpleasant game of ring-around-Smig's-rosie. As they raced down the hallways, Alexander couldn't help but notice that all of the panicking passengers they encountered were heading in the opposite direction.

"Can't be Darlipple," Ryan gasped between strides. "He's visiting his Grandmother in Geteran Wephangalandis."

"How do you know all of these people?"

"Politics is way more fun if you treat it like a professional sport!"

"Are you *sure* we're going the right way?" Smig asked as another crowd passed them.

"Yes! This is the main hall right through here!"

They burst through a set of doors to find themselves suddenly surrounded by guards brandishing an array of deadly weapons.

"What are you two doing on the boarding deck!?" an officer roared at them.

"Uhh... I could have sworn this was the main hall," Ryan stammered.

"Alexander?" a deep, familiar voice asked.

Chancellor Bulbeeyoog suddenly appeared, fully pixelated, towering over the heads of his bodyguards.

"Uh, yeah!" Smig replied. "I'm sorry, sir. We were trying to find the main deck and got lost."

"Is that Ryan Schmidtke?" Bulbeeyoog said with some annoyance in his voice.

Alexander said "Yes." at the same instant that Ryan squeaked "No."

"Okay, Colonel. I know these two. Your men can stand down."

"Return to station!" the Colonel shouted. "Secure the door!"

"Alexander, this is a delicate situation," the Chancellor admonished. "I need you and Ryan to keep quiet and stay out of the way. Understand?"

"Absolutely!" Alexander replied.

"Don't have to tell me twice!" Ryan called out, already hiding behind a column.

A series of explosions wracked the hull outside, and a monsterous, metallic clunk resounded from the far end of the boarding deck. Alexander ducked behind the column with Ryan for safety as the big double doors at the other side of the room buckled and caved in. Dust and sparks cascaded through the compromised entrance.

"Oh! Oh! It's got to be Stacy Funkletter!" Ryan said. "Watch! She's going to send in her tumbling geckaloid clowns!"

Out of the dust stormed a horde of angry space pirates. The rag-tag lot clamored into the hall, brandishing some kind of living bladed weapon that foamed at the mouth like it was rabid. They rapidly arranged themselves in a rough semi-circle across from the Chancellor's guard, who themselves, had formed ranks with guns drawn.

"Wait! Shoot!" Ryan shouted, clamping his hands to the sides of his head. "Nine people! I forgot the Dread Pirate Peter the Penisless!"

As if on cue, said Dread Pirate Peter the Penisless stooped under the gigantic entryway and entered the hall. The popcorn creatures on the ceiling fled to avoid being scraped off by the snowplow-sized brim of the scoundrel's hat as he drew himself up to his full height, which overshadowed even the Chancellor himself.

The monumental pirate flashed a wild grin, showing off a solid Rhodium tooth that was polished to a mirror finish. However, what drew the most attention was the voluminous, wiry beard that erupt-ed from his chin and flowed over his chest to such an extent that he hardly had any need to bother wearing a shirt. Yet this wasn't simple hair, for each individual strand wriggled and writhed with a mind of its own, and the tip of each one sported a formless mouth that hissed and spat little sparks of flame at random.

Swaggering into the room with footsteps that seemed to shake the whole ship, he let loose a raucous, booming laugh through the slight haze of smoke that his beard produced.

"Greetings, Mister Chancellor, sir!" he bellowed in a mocking tone. "I do hope I'm not inconveniencing ye! I am simply here to relieve ye of yer valuables, starting with yer latest, highly-prized possession: yer new concubine!"

Alexander's blood froze as the dread pirate burst into another round of laughter. This time all the strands of his beard joined in, flaring up in a bright glow of fire as their tittering cackles chorused over his thunderous chuckle.

"Oh shnipples." Ryan exclaimed.

Alexander will (maybe) return in
Smig's Gig 2: The Next Penetration
Starring Globbo! The Talking Wonder-Penis!

About the Author

KritzelMizer is a menace to society and must be stopped at all costs. Witnesses describe him as a medium-size, tan & brown, 9-banded armadillo. He is known to wear sunglasses and refuses to drink coffee like some kind of horrible, un-American goblin. He is also known to carry bad puns and as such, should be considered extremely dangerous.

We have leads tracing him to either Southern Chile, Eastern Mongolia, or the Moon. If you should encounter him, exercise extreme caution. If he should approach you, under no circumstances should you accept any offer to listen to his favorite music selections. It's all 70's Prog Rock. Not even the stuff that stoners listen to that you might vaguely recognize the name of, either. We're talking bands that only lasted long enough to make one, maybe two albums tops, like Fields (Fields, 1971) or Samurai (Green Tea, 1970 and Kappa, 1971).

In an emergency, it is suggested you toss a real-sugar Pepsi in a distant direction to distract him. When safe to do so, contact the authorities at 1-SEE-A-DILLO to report any sightings.

I wish I could blame society for this book, but society would have every right to be offended by that notion. Sure, they stuck me in a room with a wide variety of books, movies, comics, games, porn, furry porn, and an industrial strength blender, only to then act surprised and horrified when I proceeded to create the world's absolute worst smoothie, but let's be honest. I could have hucked the blender through the window to escape out into mundane mediocrity like any sane Will Sampson would have done. Really, this is all my own fault.

Acknowledgments

I would like to thank the friends who read my rough drafts.
Not only did they not run away screaming in fear or roiling in
disgust at the so-called ideas that spawned from my mind, they fed
me even worse ones. This has only increased my concerns about
them and the fact that they know where I live.

One friend in particular performed enough editing work to
practically deserve credit as ~~co-conspirator~~ co-author. They have
asked to remain anonymous, but know that this book wouldn't be
possible without them, and if I am ever compelled to testify before
Congress on this flagrant display of moral turpitude, I will out
them immediately.

It would also be remiss if I did not thank the fine folks at Fenris
Publishing for their outstanding work in bringing this project to
fruition. Special thanks to Biz for slogging through the final edits.
Correcting my grammar is a fate I would not wish on anyone.